Pebble on t|

Short stories 1

CW00494238

Penny Luker

First Published in 2010 by Bindon Books, Leyton, Cheshire, CW6 9JA
Printed by Amazon.

Edition 2 Published in 2017 (Revised)

Acknowledgements
Many thanks to everyone who has encouraged and helped me to write this book. Thanks to Winsford Writers for ideas, suggestions and reading the stories; to my family for helping to proof read the book and identifying points to ponder and to my husband David for his support.

ISBN: 9798476358589

Contents

Her Clover Cloak

When Mrs Finney attended the Sandchester Church Women's meetings, the ladies were always friendly to her, but nobody was actually her friend. It might have been because she contributed so little to any conversation. She was the type of woman you could forget was there. Nobody noticed that she'd missed two meetings, when the president of the women's group announced that Mrs Finney had left the group. The room hushed at this unexpected news, because everyone knew the Church Women's meetings were the only social events that Mrs Finney attended.

President Annabel Carson announced, 'I've debated, with myself whether I should read out Professor Finney's letter to you all, but if I don't there will only be speculation, so I'll read out the relevant part.'

She took a deep breath and lowered her voice, presumably so nobody would think she was enjoying these revelations. *Unfortunately, my wife, in her wisdom, has decided to run off with another man. She will therefore no longer be attending your group.*

Annabel paused, 'Obviously we are sorry to lose her from our group and before we go on to other business I think we should stop for our refreshments.'

How many of us thought it was out of character for Mrs Finney to run off with a man, I really couldn't say? Had we ever seen her talk to a man, let alone flirt? The noise level rose as the meeting discussed what sort of man she would have left home for.

Martha Moon, known to her friends as Moaning Martha said, 'Well if you ask me it's disgusting. How can a married woman behave like that? And the Professor is such a nice man.'

'Power to her,' replied Sylvia, 'and what d'you mean about Professor Finney? He's bloody rude and arrogant. I always wondered how she stayed married to him.'

This comment elicited a few 'tuts' from the good ladies of Sandchester, because swearing was not the done thing. By the following week the discussion turned to other things and Mrs Finney and her man were forgotten.

It was ten months later when Professor Finney telephoned me to ask if I could look after her cat.

'I've been invited to speak at Melbourne University and I thought I'd stay out there for a couple of months. Obviously I'll leave you money for food and I can leave you a key for the garage so you can wash his dishes there. He's not a friendly cat so he doesn't require any attention. Would you mind?'

'Not at all,' I replied, thinking I'd have to go there at least twice a day. What a pain.

On the first day, laden with a supply of tinned food and biscuits I opened the garage, thinking I'd be done in five minutes, but Biscuit, a tiny tabby, came and wound his body round my legs and started purring. I fed him some tinned food and some biscuits in one of those double dishes and changed his water. He ignored the tinned food and as he ate the biscuits, I noticed his bedding consisted of an old piece of sacking. That evening I returned with a flask of tea for me and a blanket and a cushion for Biscuit. I sat down on one of the garden chairs to drink my tea and Biscuit leapt onto my lap and settled down for a cuddle.

What did the Professor mean about this cat not being friendly? I thought as the little circle of fur purred gently.

The next day I shared my tea with Bert, an elderly gentleman, who'd been asked to cut the lawn. Bert looked a bit bemused by the lawnmower so we spent some time getting it going and then Bert hurtled down the garden after the powerful machine. When I came back in the evening the front lawn was cut and there was a note from Bert saying he'd do the back lawn tomorrow. Poor man; he looked very frail. Biscuit and I enjoyed an hour of each other's company and then I locked the garage and went off home. No doubt Biscuit would be out through the cat flap to relish the night air, as soon as I'd gone.

Two days later I bumped into President Annabel's son, P.C. Carson, who mentioned that Bert had been taken to hospital. He'd had a fall. That's why he'd not come back to mow the back lawn. I thought about mowing the lawn myself, and then I decided not to. I'd agreed to look after Biscuit and between ourselves I was enjoying it, but mowing the lawn would be hard work and besides Bert and I weren't being paid for our labours.

The next day I went to visit Bert in hospital.

'Don't you worry about the garden. You did the front lawn which looks fine and in the back there's a lovely little clump of clover growing in the grass. It looks really pretty.'

'You're right, there's no point my worrying. Not a lot I can do from here, is there? I remember I had clover in my garden. It grew right across the lawn; a long strip, following the line of the drain we put in.'

I promised to visit Bert again, either at the hospital, or if he was discharged, at his home.

The weather grew hot and the days lengthened. Biscuit and I spent evenings walking in the garden and I propped up the fence while he sat on it, staring out to the field beyond. He obviously loved company and must have been missing Mrs Finney. The lawn was getting long with spindles of pink and corn coloured grass growing taller than the rest. The small clump of clover was now a large patch of white which stood out against the greenness of the grass.

One morning I was sitting in the garage with a cup of tea thinking about Mrs Finney, and Biscuit was snuggled down for a sleep on my lap and I thought, *Where was she and had she really gone off with a man? This was a lady who found socializing painful and kept herself to herself.* My thoughts were interrupted by a loud banging on the garage door. Carefully lifting Biscuit and putting him back on the garden chair I went out into the bright sunlight to see P.C. Carson standing there.

'I saw your bicycle and just thought I'd say hello. How's things?' he asked.

'Everything's fine here. Bert's back is still bad. I've been thinking about Mrs Finney. She's too frightened of life to go running off with someone. The more I think about it the more I'm sure she wouldn't do that, and why didn't she take her cat? I can't believe she'd desert him when he's so loving'

'What are you saying, Mrs Sharp? Do you think something's happened to her?'

'I'm not sure, but I think something's wrong.'

'Mum's been saying pretty much the same thing. I don't suppose I can do much, but I'll see what I can find out.'

Two days later P.C. Carson came round to the garage again. 'I've a feeling you're right Mrs Sharp. No money has gone out of her bank account and her mobile phone, is switched off. It's been inactive for about a year. My boss said I can't take further action without any evidence.'

'So do you think the Professor has murdered her?' I asked as we walked through to the back garden.

'I'd have said not, except he didn't just say she'd gone, he said she'd left with someone, so if that's made up, why would he do that? The problem is she could be anywhere. I mean he might've buried her in the garden but I couldn't dig up the whole garden without it going through official channels and that's not going to happen; if only we had a clue where she might be.'

As Constable Carson was talking an idea came into my head. I told him what Bert had said about clover growing where the ground had been dug up for his drains.

'Interesting,' said Constable Carson.

That afternoon after he'd finished work, he and his brother Michael turned up at the Finney's home and I brought along some homemade lemonade and cake. I knew it would be hard work. The sun was hot and the earth was hard. They'd been digging for about an hour and were on the verge of giving up when they came across a thick plastic garden bag.

'O.K. we're going to stop here and call my boss. I don't want us messing up the scene. It may be nothing, but this is worth investigating.'

I slipped into the garage and took Biscuit's bedding and enticed him back to my house. Until this was sorted out I thought it safer that he wasn't left there in case they put him into a rescue home. He didn't seem to mind, especially as I gave him an extra large portion of his favourite biscuits.

P.C. Carson turned up at my house the next day, 'I'm afraid you were right. We found a body last night. It'll take a few days to confirm identity, but almost certainly it'll be Eileen Finney.'

Biscuit wound himself round P.C. Carson's legs, 'Ahhhh I looked for you last night and wondered where you'd got to. Oh well I suppose there's no harm in him staying here for the time being. Anyway,' he said, turning to me, 'you'll have to pop down to the station to make a statement.'

Professor Finney was arrested on his return from Australia. It turned out he hadn't been asked to speak at Melbourne University at all. He'd been diverting funds from his university for a number of years and had planned a trip to Australia. Unfortunately Mrs Finney had heard him making arrangements. When he realized that she knew what he'd been up to, he lost his temper and hit her. He claimed he hadn't meant to kill her, but I guess we'll never know.

Mrs Finney has a new resting place now in the churchyard. We planted the clover from her garden on her grave which we thought was right, because it had helped to get her justice. The Sandchester Church Women's Group were very shocked at the demise of Mrs Finney and so are raising money to build an arbour outside the church hall in her memory.

And Biscuit - well he's in charge at my house now. He's very comfortable and I just love his company.

Dare

As Sheila and Donna, walked home from school in the dark, Sheila's brain was filtering all the information she could muster. Suddenly today, Donna had decided to become her friend. Donna, who was popular with the boys, wore all the latest clothes and had loads of friends. Mostly Donna's gang just left her alone. She was boring; worked hard and did what her parents told her. She didn't have a boyfriend, hardly ever wore make up and didn't drink. Sheila did have a couple of close friends, but she knew that it wasn't wise to upset Donna, so she'd gone along with the strange new friendship. In spite of all their differences they had a similar look about them. Sheila wore her blonde hair in a single plait down her back, while Donna's was loose. They were about the same height and could have been taken for sisters.

'I'll see you tomorrow Donna. I don't go that way. It takes you through the churchyard,' said Sheila.

'Don't be such a chicken. We can both go this way and then I can get to my house and you can cut through the churchyard. It'll be quicker for you and we can spend more time together.'

'Sorry, I'm going the other way.'

'You're never frightened of ghosts are you? I thought someone as clever as you would know that's all rubbish. Go on, I dare you to go through the churchyard'

'No, I'm sure it's all rubbish. It's people alive and well, that frighten me. See you.' She called over her shoulder as she quickly marched away.

11

Donna called out after her, 'Come back, I'll walk through the churchyard with you.'

'Sorry, see you tomorrow.'

She was not her father's daughter for nothing. He'd taught her well, being an inspector in the local police force. He had told her never to go into the graveyard on her own as drug dealers hung out there sometimes and they would see her as a potential money source. He had also drummed into her to trust her instincts and that if she was feeling uncomfortable with someone to get away. She was definitely feeling uncomfortable with Donna. She couldn't understand why Donna wanted her to go into the graveyard. What was going on? She looked back but Donna was gone, so she ran home. It had been a very strange day.

At eleven that night the front doorbell rang. Inspector Willis, one of her dad's friends stood in the doorway.

'Can we speak to Sheila please?' he asked and so she came downstairs in her sensible pyjamas, wrapped up in a warm dressing gown.

'You can talk to me on my own. At sixteen, I'm sure your dad wouldn't mind,' he said.

'No, I haven't done anything wrong. He might as well be here.'

Her father sat on the sofa with her as Terry Willis asked her questions.

'Can you tell me about your day?'

'Well yes, but there's nothing that will interest you.'

'We're particularly interested in any contact you've had with Donna Lane.'

'OK, I see. Usually Donna sticks with her group of friends, but today for some reason she wanted to be my friend. I don't know why, but I went along with it, because I know what she can do if you upset her.'

'Did she ask you for anything, money, jewellery, your phone...?'

'No, but she insisted we walk home together, which I didn't really want to do, but as I said, you don't want to upset her. I always walk through the town, because it's lighter and there are people around, but when we came to Church Walk, she wanted us to go up there. I said no and she said I was scared. I said, 'See you' and marched off. I'm not allowed to go through the churchyard.'

'And you always do what your dad says?'

Sheila smiled. 'He told me about the drug dealers that work there and that seemed a good reason not to go there, besides I felt Donna was trying to manipulate me. I didn't feel that the friendship was real.'

Her dad, who'd kept quiet during the questioning, now asked the obvious question?'

'Has something happened to Donna, Terry?'

'I'm sorry to have to tell you that she was bludgeoned to death.' Her body was found in the churchyard and you Sheila, are the last person to see her alive.

'Except the murderer,' said Sheila.
***

A week later, Sheila was standing at the entrance to Church Walk.

'You don't have to do this if you don't want to,' her dad said.

'No, I will. We need to find out what happened.'

'OK,' said Inspector Willis. 'You're going to pretend to be Donna. For some reason she decided to enter the churchyard, even though that was not her direct route home. There are three of our officers already in the churchyard. Your dad will walk about twenty paces behind you and there are officers at both ends of the path. You're all wired up so just shout if anyone approaches you. We'll be filming the whole reconstruction from the church tower and we'll put it on the local TV, tomorrow night. Any questions?'

'No, let's just get it done.' 'When you're ready,' said Inspector Willis.

Sheila took a deep breath and started walking up Church Walk. It was dark and the street lights cast small pools of yellow against the pavement. As she entered the churchyard the darkness deepened.

There were no overhead lights. Sheila could feel her heartbeat quicken. Her eyes darted across the graveyard. She could dimly make out the large stones that were jutting out at assorted angles. These were the old graves. There was complete quiet. She listened for her dad's footsteps but heard none.

Suddenly she heard a girl shouting out. She held her breath. 'It's me, she wouldn't come. Dylan, I tried, but she wouldn't come. Dylan where are you? Arrrrgh. Dylan it's me.'

Sheila stood absolutely still and turned round to look where the voice was coming from. She was just in time to see Donna being hit on the head by a shadowy figure and fall to the ground. What was going on? Donna had been dead a week.

Then she heard running feet coming towards her. Her dad was shouting.

'What's wrong? Why have you stopped? Did you see something?'

'Something spooked me, but I'm all right now. Did anyone hear anything?'

Her dad checked, but none of the officers had heard a noise.

'Do you want me to go on?'

'Yes if you're up to it, but I'm going to be right behind you,' her dad said.

When they reached the end of the churchyard, Inspector Willis was there to greet them. He was scanning through the digital video.

'O.K. what happened? Did you see something? Did you remember something?' Inspector Willis asked.

Sheila knew that if she said she'd seen Donna, everyone would think she'd gone mad, but she was sure of what she'd seen. Donna had tried to persuade her to go through the churchyard, where Dylan was going to attack her. But why? She knew that somehow she needed to direct the police to Dylan Marsh. She was sure it had been him who had killed Donna.

'I'd like to go home. I'm sorry I messed up tonight but I think Donna was setting me up to be attacked. I just don't know why. Have you questioned Dylan Marsh?'

Her dad and Inspector Willis exchanged a meaningful glance.

'Why do you mention him love?' asked her dad.

'No reason really, except I caught him looking at me with absolute hatred on the day Donna died. I remembered his look while I was walking. It's probably just my imagination though, because I haven't done anything to annoy him.'

'Come on Sheila, let's get you home,' her dad said putting his arm round her.

When the police searched Dylan Marsh's home they found nothing at first and then Inspector Willis asked to look at his leather coat. It turned out that he'd wiped it down with a damp cloth but he hadn't thrown it away, because it was his favourite and he couldn't afford a new one. With forensic evidence against him, he confessed to killing Donna.

'It should've been that bitch Sheila. Her dad put my dad away. I was going to make him pay. Why should he have his family when mine is blown to bits? I was going to make him suffer, but I'm sorry I did Donna. She was my mate,' he spat out at Inspector Willis, as he was being led away.

'I don't know how you knew it was Dylan, but we might not have got there without your input. Sorry my job put you in danger,' her dad said to her later.

'Well it was also your job that saved my life. Anyway, I don't think I'll ever go in that churchyard again,' Sheila said with a smile.

But the girl in the churchyard continued to shout and was sometimes seen by people passing by. Some believe that those who die a violent death, can leave an imprint on this earth, like an old fashioned video recording, which plays again and again.

Days Like That

Edna had known it would be bad day as soon as the postman knocked on her door to complain about the gate. The faulty latch had taken a chunk out of his finger and he'd left blood spots all over her letters.

Then she'd tripped over her own feet and landed awkwardly on her elbow.

Drat, she thought, *I've promised to drive Mrs. Large to the hospital today.*

Her elbow ached, but there was nothing she could do, so she took a painkiller.

Mrs. Large, who was a lady who suited her name, struggled to get the seatbelt on. After a two hour wait at the hospital Edna's elbow was throbbing again.

'Not a very comfortable car, is it? It's so small,' was the 'thank you' she received from Mrs. Large.

The day can only get better, Edna thought as she drove to the supermarket and then the accident happened.

'You stupid woman. Why don't you look where you're going?' The man said as he wrenched open her car door.

'I was looking where I was going. Ever heard of signalling? I presume you intended to turn left.' Edna retaliated.

'If you'd have been driving at the correct distance behind, it wouldn't have mattered. It's always the fault of the car behind. Don't you even know that? Bloody women drivers!'

Edna knew she had to take control of the situation. *You could only be intimidated if you let people treat you like that,* she thought. She took several deep breaths and when she looked up she realized that she recognised the man.

'Good grief, it's not the dishy Reverend Albert Connor from the television is it? I didn't recognise you in your jeans and foul temper. Well I never. This'll be one to tell the W.I.'

She could see Albert was taken aback to be recognised.

'I hardly think it's something to go bragging about; doing thousands of pounds worth of damage, through incompetent driving.'

Edna smiled, 'Oh I don't know 'How I banged the vicar' would make quite a good headline, especially regarding a celebrity like yourself.'

'What I want to know is, are you admitting liability?' Albert asked.

'My insurance company's instructions are to never admit anything, so I most certainly am not. Perhaps we should exchange details.'

It didn't seem fair to deny responsibility for something that legally was her fault, but he really was a very unpleasant, patronising young man.

The Reverend Albert Connor gave a sigh and changed his mind.

'Look let's not get drawn into all this legal stuff. I can probably mend my car. Shall we just call it quits?'

'Well now that's much more civilized,' Edna replied. 'Although to be honest I quite fancy having your details,' she said with a cheeky smile.

Albert got into his car and drove away rather quickly, *'He really thought I was after him,'* she

18

laughed to herself. '*Why he's young enough to be my grandson.*'

The Choice

Jo threw back the bedcovers and went to get a glass of water. She couldn't sleep. There was no doubt that Carl had given her an ultimatum earlier today.

'So are you going to take the job? You'll be away on tour for months.' Carl had kissed her and run his hand through her hair. It made a shiver run down her spine.

'I don't want to leave you, but it really is a fantastic opportunity. It won't come again.'

'I know, I know, but how can we survive as a couple if we're never together?'

Jo had stepped away from his caresses. 'I just need a little thinking time. I've worked hard for so many years and this has been my dream, to dance in a real production. I can't just give it up like that.'

'Well I'm an opportunity that won't come again too. Just remember that when you're making your decision.' Carl had jumped onto his bike and roared noisily out of Delamere Forest car park leaving her standing in silence by her old battered mini.

Jo drank some water and stretched her tall slender body slowly. She wandered round the small flat in bare feet. The cold of the floor was comforting. Like others who had grown up in the children's home, her family was the group of friends that had shared so many years of childhood. Physically they'd not always been together but kept in touch by mobile and e-mail. Of her six close friends Emily had always been there for her. She'd phone her tomorrow and ask her advice.

Having made a decision, however small, Jo trundled off back to bed in the hope of sleep.

The following day she downed a cup of coffee and made her way to the college practice room, which was booked for 8.30 a.m. After two hours of hard work she felt happy as she wiped her face with a towel. Ballet made her feel so alive. The music transformed her into a paintbrush, weaving pictures across the room, sometimes quick sharp strokes and other times, languid long lines of pure grace.

As soon as she'd showered, and changed into the student uniform of jeans and tee shirt, she found a quiet place on the grass to sit down and call Em.

'Part of me knows I have to take this opportunity, but what if I lose him? It's so wonderful to have someone who's mine. I couldn't bear it if we split.'

'O.K. let's try it the other way around. Suppose he was offered a job in America, teaching at a top school, perhaps with a promotion; would you tell him to take it or stay where he is and be with you?' said Emily.

'Well I'd want him to stay, but I'd have to encourage him to do what was best for him, or he'd hate me later on.'

'I think you've just answered your own question then, haven't you? If you don't take this chance, you'll come to resent him. If he loves you, you'll find ways to see each other.'

'Thanks for talking it through Em. I'll let you know what happens. Speak soon.'

Carl came round that evening and Jo cooked him a simple pasta meal. He said nothing about the job throughout the evening and although Jo knew she had to tell him her decision, she didn't want to spoil the evening.

Later he drew her towards him but she didn't feel like making love. Pulling away she said, 'I've thought long and hard about the dancing contract and …'

'Don't tell me you're going to take it. Please don't. It will be the biggest mistake of your life.'

'What d'you mean?'

'I mean if you're taking it, that's us done. I'm not hanging around waiting for you.'

'We'll still be able to meet up. I'll travel back when I get a day off and you can come and visit at weekends.'

Carl stood up and picked up his leather jacket from the back of a chair. 'Nope, that's not my scene. If you're going away, that's it. Good luck with your dancing. You'll need it because you're going to be a sad, lonely, old biddy.' The front door slammed and he was gone.

Jo left the washing up piled in the sink and went to climb under her duvet. She felt like a knife had cut her in half. Effectively she'd just got rid of the first man she'd ever loved and for all she knew the last. The tears fell freely and she knew she'd made the wrong decision. It must be. The pain was so bad but strangely she was asleep within minutes.

The next day she was up at six. She had another early practice and she knew she had to clear up before she went out. Years in care had taught her that you kept the daily routines going when your world was falling apart. It was a coping strategy.

In the solitude of the studio the music took over and Jo gave herself to the practice and routines she had to learn. Inside her body felt stiff and awkward. She knew she was just rubbish. 'Why had she sent Carl away?' But as she danced she caught sight, of the graceful ballerina that pirouetted in the mirror. It was a shock to realize that it was her dancing. She continued the routine and as she did so she could feel her body stretch and move to the music.

She drew herself up to her full height as the dance ended and knew she'd made the right decision. She'd never be a sad, lonely, old biddy while she had the ability to dance.

Clapping startled her as she finished the dance.

'I just had a feeling you might be needing a friend,' said Em.

Jo ran towards her and gave her a hug. 'Who could have a better family? Give me ten minutes to shower and change.'

'O.K. and then let's go to Starbucks.' Em called after her and when they arrived at the café Jo couldn't help but smile. All their friends were there.

April Showers

April stretched her painful limbs and did her exercises as usual before she left her bed. The pain was worse in the morning in all kinds of ways. There was the dull ache of the joints in her legs, which lessened as the day grew older, but there was also the morning shock of loss. Each new day, after sleep had taken her to happy forgetfulness, she awoke to overwhelming grief that punched her in the stomach.

Who would have thought how different her life would be in the space of a year? She remembered back to last April. Her mother had been busy preparing a wonderful buffet for her birthday, while she was vacuuming their cottage and getting the music together for the party. All her friends were coming over in the evening including her boyfriend, Max.

The evening had been a great success and Max had suggested that they should get engaged soon. She'd noticed her mother's slight hesitation at the news, but it had been so quickly covered with congratulations that she'd thought she'd imagined it.

What a happy summer they'd spent. The sun shone on long leisure filled days whilst Max and she explored canals, took country walks, visited little pubs and rambled around local lakes.

Then one day her mum said, 'Could you help me with the shopping on Friday night instead of Saturday morning? I want to go to an art class on Saturday.'

'Of course mum. No problem.'

When she told Max, he said, 'Don't you remember it's Silvia and Bob's party on Friday? We promised we'd go.'

'I'll only be about an hour. Surely we can go later. Mum does a lot to look after me and for that matter she cooks quite a few meals for you every week. The least we can do is help with the shopping.'

'I tell you what, as I don't want to let down Silvia and Bob, I'll go on to the party and you can join me when you get away.'

April stared at him. Was he joking? What difference did an hour make when going to a party? But he hadn't been. April and her mum enjoyed their shopping trips. They always took a list but on the way round the shelves they both slipped little treats into the basket and ended up spending way more than they intended. On Friday night they set off, with April already wearing her party clothes. Her mother drove the car to the supermarket, in her usual steady manner, but a car full of youngsters came round the corner on the wrong side of the road.

Just one moment of not concentrating and the world upended. April remembered very little until she woke in a hospital bed, in pain and wearing a lot of bandages. A gentle blonde police woman told her about the accident and that was the first time she felt the jolt of grief physically blast through her body. She lay back on the bed with crazy images darting through her mind. Then her phone rang and the police woman handed it to her from her handbag. It was her best friend Jenny.

'Hey April, where are you? You're missing a great party. Hurry up.'

April explained what had happened and Jenny rushed straight over. Fleetingly April wondered why Max hadn't come with her but all she could really think about was her mum and how she would never see her again. Jenny turned up the next morning with pyjamas, a wash bag, some squash and fruit.

'I've been talking to the doctor and she seems to think you'll be home in a few days, as long as someone can look after you, so I thought I might come and stay until you're back walking.'

April squeezed her hand. She knew she'd be in safe hands and she didn't want to go back to the house alone. Max came round for the first time on the day she arrived home. He hugged her awkwardly as he sat down beside her.

'I'm so sorry about your mum and your accident. Jenny has promised me she'll look after you and you know if you need anything you can call me.'

April's brain became alert. She could hear from the tone of his voice he was dreading speaking to her.

'What's wrong?' she asked, as Jenny left the room with a look of loathing for Max.

'Well I've met someone else. I know it's really bad timing, but I don't want to tell you lies. She was at Silvia's party and well I just couldn't stop myself. You know I'll always be your friend. It's just one of those things.'

'Thanks for coming round to tell me in person Max. Will you see yourself out? I really need a little rest.' April didn't cry until he'd left and even then she felt she was crying for her mum and not for Max. Jenny came back in carrying steaming hot mugs of carrot soup.

'More fool him. What we need is some comfort food. I've made an apple pie and custard for pudding.

26

Let's just slob out today and tomorrow we'll try out the wheel chair and go for a walk; sorry, I mean a breath of fresh air.'

For six weeks Jenny nursed April and stayed on until April could manage on her own. She encouraged their friends to visit and gradually April began to sort herself out. As she physically recovered she knew she had to keep busy. Her mother wouldn't have wanted her to give up. She decided to decorate the house and have a new bathroom fitted. Andy, the plumber, asked her out, but although flattered, she wasn't ready. At any other time April would have noticed Andy's quiet good looks.

One day in January, April went out into the garden and found it looking sad. It was missing her mum as much as she was. She set to work digging over the ground, preparing the way for the beans. It was surprising how much better she felt spending some time outdoors. In February, Silvia and Bob came over to help her plant out the autumn variety of raspberry canes. In March she planted tomatoes in pots and seed potatoes in trays. The greenhouse and garden started to feel loved again. Violet and yellow crocuses showed their heads amongst the grass as they'd done last year.

Life seemed to be getting back to normal when one Sunday afternoon at the end of March, Jenny and April were having tea and cake and the front door bell chimed. April opened the door to find Max standing there.

'I hear you're back on your feet and I just thought I'd pop in and see how you are.'

'I'm busy Max, but thanks for calling. Please go back to your girlfriend.'

'Well that's just it. We've split up and I know I made a huge mistake breaking up with you. Hey can I come in so we can talk properly?'

'We've nothing to say. I lost my mother and you dumped me. When you know that someone can abandon you at the time when your world crashes, there's no future. I'm sorry you've split up with your girlfriend, but as I said, I'm busy and I'd like you to leave.'

What had she seen in him? she wondered as he walked down the path.

Half an hour later the doorbell chimed again. But this time an older man stood at the door.

'Good afternoon. I recognise you from photographs your mother sent me. I know you don't know me, but I'm your father, Gerald Eames. May I have five minutes of your time?'

April was glad that Jenny had come round. She felt it wasn't wise to be on her own with this stranger.

'I've been abroad or I'd have come sooner. I made your mother a promise, that if anything ever happened to her I'd get in touch. I've just found out and I'm so sorry. Your mum was a lovely lady.'

'Is that why you deserted her?'

'Ouch. I expect I deserve that. We split up before she knew about you and it seemed false to get back together for the sake of a baby. But I did send her money until she went back out to work and she didn't want me in your lives.'

'I'm not sure that I do.'

'As I've totally neglected to be any kind of father I don't blame you, but perhaps we could go for a meal sometime. We might find that we want to be in touch, but if at any time you decide you really don't, that would be fine. And I want you to know that if ever you need any help or support you only have to ask. I've written my address and telephone number here and I'll leave it to you to ring me. Now that your mum's not here you might find it handy to have some family around.'

When he'd left April said, 'What an afternoon! First Max and then Gerald. Who do they think they are?' She didn't want to think of Max or Gerald Eames.

'Well Gerald might've just been following your mum's wishes. He didn't seem too bad,' said Jenny.

Two weeks later in April, Jenny came round to help plant onions, broad beans, peas and lettuce. The day had started with the sun shining through the windows and April had woken knowing that her mum wasn't with her. She still felt sad, but the shock was lessening. She stretched her legs slowly and the aches eased. There was so much to do with all that planting. Last year she'd have been helping her mum, but this year Jenny would be helping her. She quickly showered and was on her second cup of coffee when Jenny arrived. They started work and were chatting and laughing, hard at work, when it started to drizzle.

'I suppose we'd better go indoors,' Jenny said.

'You go in if you want to.' April took a deep breath and smelled the fresh air. It was so sweet. The warm rain on her face was comforting and the feel of earth in her hands was like being in touch with life again. As the custard yellow daffodils nodded their heads in the breeze April lifted her arms to the sky and ran round the garden. She'd miss her mother for a long time to come but no-one could take away her memories.

Jenny smiled at her friend, threw her hands in the air and also started to dance in rain.

'Have you gone mad?' April laughed.

'Only as mad as you.'

April hugged her friend. 'Thanks for being everything a friend should be. If it hadn't been for you I wouldn't have come through this past year.'

'Don't be daft,' Jenny said all embarrassed, 'course you would.'

'I made a decision today,' April said. 'I'm going to go for a meal with my father. I want to know my parents' story and you never know, I may even get to like him. What do you think?'

'I think that's a great idea and I made a decision today too. I'm going to have my bathroom done. It doesn't really need it but I rather fancy your plumber,' laughed Jenny, relieved that April was coming back to life, even if the two of them were drenched to the skin.

The Little Red Book

I found the book of handwritten poems and notes in the drawer beside what had been my Grandfather's bed. It was the key to unlock our family secrets.

Andy and I moved into my Grandfather's house two months after he died. It was a beautiful old house, large with high ceilings and big rooms. The whole place wanted redecorating and the kitchen and bathrooms needed to be completely stripped out, but we could do the work at our own pace, because everything was functional. Andy was practical and we'd enjoy doing the place up.

Mum and Dad came over with soup and rolls on moving day, which was extremely welcome.

'You'll need to get rid of this table. It's seen better days,' Mum commented.

'Actually I think all it needs is a good rub down to get the grime off. It's quite old but pine like this could look really great,' replied Andy.

Dad and Andy went into a discussion about what needed to be done and Mum smiled and rolled her eyes towards the ceiling. I was aware how the atmosphere had changed now that Grandfather was no longer with us. It sounds awful to say but the house seemed happier. There was always a sense of gloom when we visited. He obviously loved us all but he rarely laughed. He'd talk seriously about important matters and his house was full of books, but I never remember him having a chuckle.

Sorting this house out was going to take months, perhaps years, but I had a good feeling it was going to make a lovely family home. I stroked my gently expanding stomach. We'd have survived in the flat where we started our married life, but it was going to be wonderful to open the back door and have a garden.

As my parents went to leave, having helped us get all the basics sorted, I gave them both a hug.

'Thank you so much for letting us have this house. We could never have afforded something so beautiful.'

'Lottie, you're our only daughter and it'll be lovely to have you living closer. Anyway we like where we are and your mother's not that keen to live here.'

'But why?' asked Andy.

'Not sure really,' Mum replied. 'I do love this place but there's something about this house. I can't put my finger on it. It's great you don't feel it and as long as you're happy then everything's fine. I'm sure you two, or should I say three, will make it into a happy home.'

It was later that night as we lay exhausted in each other's arms that Andy confided in me.

'I know how your mum feels. There's something not quite right about this place. Don't get me wrong, I'm not feeling evil vibes or anything like that, just that the house is out of kilter.'

That night I dreamed of a fragile ghost who walked through the house in a floaty muslin dress. She followed me around as I looked after my baby, singing lullabies. She wore the prettiest satin shoes with big floppy pink ribbons tied in bows. We all went and sat on a rug on the large neat lawn and she made a daisy chain. It took me a moment to realise we were sitting in our garden, although it looked slightly different.

Sunlight streaming through the old sash windows woke me and I could hear birdsong in the garden. My mind was in conflict. It had been a warm feeling that I'd met my baby but I wanted to know who the girl was. She seemed so real.

I dressed in a pretty maternity top and jeans and brushed my dark hair until it shone. Although I was beginning to feel like a waddling penguin I still wanted to look good for Andy. He was tall and strong with the warmest brown eyes and when he walked into a room I often felt shocked at how much I loved him. I went downstairs and laid out the breakfast things. Where was Andy? Then I saw that the French windows in the large sitting room were slightly open and slipped out to take a look. He was pacing and counting along the side of the house. When he reached the end he turned, saw me and jogged back to me. In his eyes I saw excitement.

'I know what's wrong with the house. C'mon, I'll show you. This house has a bigger downstairs than upstairs, but from the outside it looks as if it should be the same.'

'Are you sure?'

'Yes that's what I've been doing, while you've been having your beauty sleep. The house is ten paces longer downstairs than upstairs. I've also been looking at the brickwork and there are two bricked up windows up there. Can you see them? Oh they've been expertly done but if you look closely you can see where they once were. We've got a secret room.' He couldn't help the eagerness in his voice.

Andy almost ran upstairs. 'C'mon Lottie, let's see if we can find it.'

In my head I was questioning why Grandfather would have a secret room. I climbed the stairs carefully and went into the room at the back of the house, to find Andy tapping on the end wall. I sat on Grandfather's single metal bed. The mattress was surprisingly comfortable. Andy's taps on the wall suddenly changed as he moved to the right hand side of the wall. They made a different sound. He checked again and looked at me confirming that we could both tell the difference.

'Before you rip off the wallpaper and start knocking the doorway through have you thought what might be on the other side?'

'I think there'll be an empty room. People used to close down rooms and brick up windows to save tax, but you're right there may be something more sinister, although your Grandfather didn't seem like a potential Crippen to me. I'm going to knock it down and then I'll go in first. I don't want you to have any nasty surprises.'

As Andy found the necessary tools, I idly opened the drawer next to Grandfather's bed. It was there I found a dark red leather book with handwritten pages. Inside the front cover was an inscription. *This book belongs to Lydia Harvey.* How strange I thought. Harvey was the family name but who was Lydia?

I read some of the entries.

Today I was ill again. I don't remember it but I fell and shook and screamed. I made noises not suitable for a young lady. Father says I must stay in my room until the illness passes, but he knows I can't control these episodes. He says if they call the doctor they will take me away and he doesn't want to lose me. I don't mind being here. Albert brought me my lunch and stayed and played Ludo with me. I'm lucky to have such a kind brother.

My heart beat faster. Albert was my Grandfather's name. It looked as though Lydia was his sister.

Then there was a poem.

I saw a robin redbreast,
He sang his song to me
But then a door slammed
And he flew into a tree.

If I can come tomorrow,
And I am on the mend
I'll sing to the Robin
To come and be my friend.

It was a simple poem, written by a child, but it opened a little window into her world. I wanted to know more about Lydia. I knew she was important.

Meanwhile Andy had ripped off some wallpaper and a pile of plaster lay crumbled on the floor. He was through to the doorway.

'Just give me a minute, to see everything's alright.'

I waited.

'It's fine. Come on through.'

The room was dim with the only light coming from Grandfather's room. Andy hooked up a portable light that he used for working in the loft. It gave a gentle glow that left the corners in shadow. The room smelled musty from being locked up for so long. It was a girl's bedroom. There was yellowed wallpaper sprinkled with tiny faded roses, a single bed with a patchwork bedspread covering the mattress. To one side of the room was a bathroom area. It had a tired looking curtain screening it from the rest of the room.

There was no bath or shower but a toilet and small basin. The room contained two chairs, a table and a large cupboard, which still held board games and artist pads, crayons and dried up paints. The book case was packed with books. Some were beautifully illustrated. It was like stepping into a time warp. In the wardrobe there still hung clothes, no bigger than for a child of twelve or thirteen. There were several pairs of shoes. One pair was made of satin, with pink ribbon bows. We spent a good hour exploring and Andy came over and hugged me, obviously feeling the same as me; that we were intruding into someone's life.

I called my mum as soon as we left the room and she knew nothing of Lydia. Later that week I went to the County Record's Office to look up the church's inventory on births and deaths. I needed to know about Lydia Harvey. Somehow she felt a part of me. It took two hours before I found the entry. She had lived for just twelve years and was buried with my great-grandparents. I took myself off to the churchyard. It was hard to visit the place where we had so recently buried Grandfather. The memorial cross made of grey granite stood above the grave I knew to be my great grandparents. I examined the stone. There was no sign of Lydia's name. Then I bent down to the side of the square plinth and pushed down the grass and there engraved was the name Lydia, but with no dates or messages.

I felt so sad that this child had been hidden away because of her condition and that even in death the shame of her epilepsy had caused her to be buried so discreetly. What could be done to put things right?

Now two years later we have re-established the lawn and the garden has masses of bluebells in the spring. Andy has made a bird table and hung feeders and we've spotted thirty seven different species so far, including a robin. I like to think that it's a descendant of Lydia's robin. Inside there's a new kitchen and modern bathroom and the lounge has pale walls, big earth brown sofas and a large screen television.

We've redecorated Lydia's room, opened up the windows again and added a small en-suite. It's still a young girl's bedroom. Sometimes I feel as if we're sharing the room, but it isn't a menacing feeling. It's more like a guardian angel watches over our Mollie.

The little red book is in my bedside drawer and I read it now and again. That Lydia only lived for twelve years saddens me, as it must have done my Grandfather; to know that if she'd been born in a different time she could have lived an ordinary life and may not have died so young, but there are things that we cannot change. My Mum, always a positive person, pointed out that from what Lydia had written she was a loved daughter and sister and had been treated kindly. I suppose we can't ask for much more than that. On one page near the end of the book she wrote:

> The best birthday ever is what I've just had.
> Spent with my family and not feeling sad.
> With pretty pink ribbons tied in my hair
> And pretty pink bows on the shoes that I wear.

We've mounted some of Lydia's pictures that we found in her cupboard and printed some of her poems and put them in beautiful frames. They are a part of our home and our way of celebrating her life. Andy thinks I'm mad to believe that she might still be here in some way, but sometimes I catch Mollie smiling at something I cannot see, and if Lydia *is* here then she's welcome.

The White Feather

'I don't know what's gone wrong between you two, but I wish you'd make friends again,' Stephanie said.

'There's nothing wrong between us,' said her father.

Ben was silent.

'Ben, did you have a present for your Granddad?'

Ben slid off the chair and went to his room without speaking and then reappeared and placed a beautiful white feather in front of his Granddad.

Dan's face turned almost as white as the feather, but he managed a smile and said, 'Thank you, Ben.'

Stephanie glared at her dad, 'Well I think it's beautiful Ben. Such a lovely present to give your Granddad and if you've been naughty I'm sure he'll forgive you.'

'I've not been naughty.'

They ate the meal almost in silence. Stephanie tried to get her son and dad to talk to each other, but nothing worked. In the end she switched the radio on, which was tuned to the local station.

'The police are appealing for witnesses to a vicious attack on an elderly lady. Mrs. Belcher was brutally attacked yesterday as she walked home from the shops and her handbag was stolen. She's recovering in hospital. She was found unconscious in Vanguard Street, just two minutes from her home. Anyone who saw anything suspicious should contact....'

'Oh poor Mrs. Belcher. How dreadful to hurt an old woman,' said Stephanie.

'It's disgraceful,' said Dan.

'I like Mrs. Belcher. She always talks to me. My teacher says people who see bullying and don't speak up are as bad as the person who does the bullying.'

'Well, yes, I suppose they are in a way,' said Stephanie.

'Except they haven't thought about hurting someone, have they? Perhaps they just don't want to get involved,' said Dan.

'Well I don't suppose anyone will come forward from round here,' said Stephanie. 'They'll be too scared of the thugs that did it. Anyway did you two enjoy your trip to the library yesterday?'

The afternoon passed pleasantly enough and Ben and Dan managed to speak to each other politely, but there was none of the banter and jokes that usually passed between them. When it was time to leave Dan made sure that he picked up the white feather and promised to call next week.

Dan walked home slowly. He kept to the main road, which was safer, but his mind whirled and churned. What should he do? If he told the police that he'd seen Rory Prentice and Wayne Jackson attack Mrs. Belcher he'd not only put himself at risk, he'd put Stephanie and Ben at risk as well. He might be able to defend himself but Ben and his mum would be vulnerable. And now his dearest and only grandchild was angry with him for not speaking out.

They'd been walking over the bridge and although were quite a way from Mrs. Belcher, their view had been clear. He'd been going to help her, but when he saw the boys leave and a stranger bend down to her, he'd led Ben home and made him promise not to tell anyone what they'd seen. He felt the fluffiness of the feather against his hand in his pocket and he wished he could cry out loud, but of course he wouldn't do that. At that moment he passed the telephone box. He could at least give the police the names of the thugs – anonymously. Without entering the box he could see the phone had been ripped from the wall as it hung limply, but the phones in the railway station would work. He turned round and marched with purpose back towards the station.

Twenty minutes later he felt a bit better. The police now knew who had hurt Mrs. Belcher and they could probably find some evidence to link the boys to the crime. Now all he needed to do was to get Ben to see that there were times to keep quiet.

The next morning Dan had his tea and cereal listening to the local radio. The announcer for the news came on and said that two boys had been arrested for the attack on Mrs. Belcher but had been released without charge. The police were appealing for the man who called them with information to phone back.

The phone rang and when Dan picked it up he heard Ben. 'Did you call them Granddad? Did you call the police?'

'Yes Ben, but I did it anonymously. It's not just me I'm frightened for. It's you and your mum. I know you don't understand but I love you both so much.'

'I do understand. I told dad I didn't want him to go back and fight in the war, but he said, we can't make the world the place we want to live in, unless we stand up for what's right. I want to go to the police station Granddad.'

'I'm coming round to talk this through.'

Dan picked up the photograph of his daughter on her wedding day. There she stood by her soldier

40

husband, who was now out of touch as he was on a tour of duty in Afghanistan. Suddenly he knew his grandson was right. What sort of world would it become if decent people stood by and let old ladies get beaten up? He didn't want Ben growing up in that world. He picked up the phone and spoke to the Inspector in charge of the case.

'What made you change your mind about being a witness?' she asked.

'It was my grandson, Ben. He gave me a white feather, which was a sign of cowardice, given to those who wouldn't fight in the First World War. We'd been reading a story about it at the library.'

'I see,' she said. 'We'll be round to pick you and your grandson up.'

'No, Inspector. I'm going to pick him up and we'll be there in half an hour. I don't want police cars round their house.'

The door was open when he arrived and Ben was waiting for him with his coat on. Stephanie was standing there with her coat on too. 'Come on you two, let's get going. We'll get through this together. I know we're all a bit frightened but I think the people round here will look out for us. Even kids that mess about are shocked that anyone could hurt Mrs. Belcher.'

'Sorry about the feather, Granddad.'

'Don't be Ben. I'll always treasure it.'

Pebble On The Beach

Simon let the sand tickle his feet. He was sheltered from the sun by a hat and brightly coloured shirt. It was good being on the beach but it reminded him of days with his mum and he felt sad.

'Are you on your own child?' A voice drifted towards him.

He looked up and saw a little old lady, dressed all in grey standing a few feet away. Her hair was in a bun with tendrils falling out.

'I don't usually stop and talk to strange children but you were looking rather sad.'

'I'm not on my own. Look my dad is just there and I'm not allowed to talk to people I don't know.'

'Well that's very sensible and I won't come any nearer you, but I just wondered if you are missing someone, because if you are I may be able to help.'

'You can't help. I miss my mum but she's gone to heaven and can't come back.'

'Did your mum love you very much?'

'Yes, she did. She used to hug me all the time and she used to kiss me goodnight when she read me a story.'

'Well let me tell you a secret. When we love someone in this world, we still love them when we pass to the next. Love doesn't just stop because our body stops working. You know that if your mum was here today she'd give you a hug and a kiss, and if you try hard you might be able to feel them'

'I have tried hard. It doesn't work.'

'Well you see that beautiful pebble in front of you... no the pinkish one...yes that's the one; if you pick it up and hold it in your hand, close your eyes and think of one of your mum's hugs, you should be able to feel it.'

Simon looked over to his dad and gave him a wave. His dad waved back. Should he trust this old woman, who was standing with her lace up boots on the sand? He took a deep breath. His dad was obviously keeping an eye on him, so he held the pebble tightly and closed his eyes. Sure enough he felt warm arms give him a hug and heard his mother's voice. The words weren't clear to begin with but then he heard her say,

'When your dad ruffles your hair he's giving you a hug in his own way and when he gives you a mock punch on the shoulder that's a kiss. You are our lovely son and as I can't be with you now, you and your dad are going to have to look after each other. I love you son. Always.'

Slowly Simon opened his eyes and saw his dad waving him back for the sandwiches he'd prepared earlier. They didn't look as good as his mum's had, as the bread was cut unevenly but he'd put in his favourite tuna and salad cream filling in. Simon was about to say thank you to the old lady, when he realized she'd gone. He looked along the wide beach, which stretched for miles, but she was nowhere to be seen. He pulled his feet out of the sand and pattered over to where his dad was sitting.

His dad gave him a mock punch on the shoulder and handed him a chunky sandwich. Simon smiled. He was lucky to have such a great dad.

'These are my favourite sandwiches,' he said and saw his dad really smile for the first time in ages.

'Hey did you see that old lady I was talking to?'

'No, who was she?'

'I don't know, but I could've shouted for you if she'd been nasty. Anyway she told me that mum still loves us even though she's not here and she said if I hold this pebble and close my eyes I'll still be able to feel mum's hugs.'

'Did she now?' Simon's dad was looking along the beach, scanning all the people there.

'But then the strangest thing happened; when I opened my eyes she was gone and I looked down the beach and I couldn't see her anywhere. How weird is that?'

'Very odd. I hope she didn't upset you.'

'No, dad. Anyway it worked and I did feel one of mum's hugs.'

'What did this woman look like?'

'Well she was about a hundred, with her hair in a bun and she was all dressed in grey, except for lace up boots. That was strange too. Fancy wearing lace ups on a beach! And she had kind eyes and a lovely smile.'

'Maybe you dropped off and had a dream.'

'No I didn't, and you must've seen her. She was standing only a few feet away when you waved at me.'

Simon's dad became very busy packing up all the food and then they went off together to explore some rock pools.

That evening Simon's dad sat down deflated, wondering if his son was suffering some kind of mental problem, which would be totally natural, considering what he'd been through. He'd only seen his son sitting on the beach alone. There'd been no old lady. To keep himself busy he took out all the photograph albums

44

and started flicking through them. This was a bit of an addiction because he missed his wife so much and he pretended she was still there as he looked at her photos.

He was putting them back in the cupboard when he noticed a very old album stuck at the back. He picked it up and flipped through the pages. His eyes fell on a black and white photo of an old lady with her hair falling out of a bun. It was impossible to tell what colour she was dressed in but she was wearing black lace up boots.

He trundled off to bed with all sorts of thoughts churning in his mind.

The following morning he was woken by Simon jumping on the bed.

'It's her! It's her! This is the lady I saw yesterday,' Simon said as he shoved the album towards his dad.

Rubbing sleep from his eyes, Simon's dad looked at the same picture he'd found the night before.

'Maybe son. Let's get some breakfast shall we?'

As they sat together he realized he had the old Simon back; a happy animated young lad, full of a child's enthusiasm. He didn't understand what had happened on the beach yesterday; how his wife's grandmother could've been there, but somehow, someone or something had brought his son comfort. He ruffled Simon's hair. Today was a new day. The sun was shining and he knew that he and Simon were going to be happy again.

The Life and Crimes of Neville Grimes

Neville Grimes was not a pleasant man. Nor was he typical or normal in any way. He started his working life at sixteen, took all the overtime he could and saved. He invested and took out insurance schemes and treasured his assets. Friday nights he enjoyed the most, because he indulged in counting up how much money he was worth.

'Are you doing anything nice this weekend, Mr Grimes?' Tracy, the office junior asked.

'Nothing special.'

'Haven't you got a girlfriend then?'

'No Tracy, I don't want any old baggage. I want a perfect woman and when I'm rich I shall buy her.'

'You can't buy a woman. Women can't love to order you know. Oh are you having me on?' she laughed.

'Well that's where you're wrong, Tracy. Money will buy you everything you want, as long as you have enough of it and I save almost everything I earn.'

'How do you manage that? After rent, food, clothes, paying for the car and holidays, there's not much left. I mean I know you probably earn double what I earn, but even so.'

'I pay my mum £5 a week, that's how.'

'But how can she feed you on that and she makes you up scrumptious lunch boxes. They alone would cost more than that?'

'She's happy with that arrangement, so don't worry yourself about it.'

In fact Mrs Grimes was far from happy but she found her son so intimidating that she daren't ask for more. It wasn't just that she had to eek out her meagre pension to support them both, it was his demands for an immaculate home. His cheap clothes had to be ironed to perfection and when he was in a bad mood he could make such cutting remarks.

A couple of years later Tracy left the office and Mr Grimes remained.

When he reached the age of fifty five, he'd saved well over a million pounds. He felt the time had come to enjoy himself. He had his teeth straightened and whitened; his hair dyed and bought new expensive clothes and a sports car. He said good-bye to his mother and moved into a luxury apartment. His mother immediately put the house on the market and moved into a one bed-roomed flat in sheltered accommodation, so that he could never move back.

Within a week he realized that he needed a woman to clean and cook for him. He was very particular and didn't want to ruin his hands. Nor did he wish to rush to choose a partner, because the perfection he was looking for would take a little time to find, so he advertised for a home help. The only applicant was Carole, a delicate, young woman, whom he interviewed in depth.

'Right the jobs yours. Start Monday,' he said.

'Before I agree to take the job you need to explain the wages and hours of work,' replied Carole.

A little taken aback by the confidence this girl showed and having no idea what to pay her, he said £2 an hour, three hours a day, which he felt was indeed generous.

'Mr Grimes the minimum wage for my age group is £4.77 per hour. Let me be very clear I certainly wouldn't take the job of looking after an old man, cleaning up this sort of mess *and* cooking for him for that wage. If you want me to do the job I'll do it for £7.50 an hour.'

Now Mr Grimes was horrified at the attitude of this young woman but far more horrified at the cost. He was about to show her out when he realized that he'd have to start doing housework and cooking.

'OK, I'll agree to those terms on a month's trial basis,' he replied, intending to use the month to find someone cheaper. Fleetingly he wondered if he'd been a little stingy with his mother but the thought passed quickly and certainly before he considered apologising or giving her some of his wealth.

Having sorted out his housekeeping problems he settled down to finding himself a perfect woman. He had so much money he was sure he could buy just about anyone. He'd have the choice of hundreds, but where could he meet them? He went to several clubs but no-one spoke to him and so he called up an escort agency.

'I want a blonde lady, with an hour glass body, who doesn't talk too much and doesn't use the word 'old' in any conversation with me.'

'We'll send you Cindy round tonight at seven pm.'

Mr Grimes paid the agency and then privately offered Cindy a little extra for services above and beyond those supplied by the agency. It didn't occur to Mr Grimes that being inexperienced at his age would be a problem and Cindy although quite revolted by the strange Mr Grimes soon assessed the situation and did her best to help him. At the end of the evening, he didn't want to look at Cindy and he decided he certainly didn't want to see her again.

The next evening the 'Anytime' agency sent another girl. And so it went on, night after night. None of the girls measured up to Mr Grimes' idea of perfection. He didn't quite appreciate that he didn't measure up for them either. Although now old enough to be a granddad he'd missed out all those years of living. He still thought of himself as young and attractive. He felt sure that his smart new teeth made him quite desirable. It was a shame Tracy wasn't about nowadays, he thought, quite forgetting she wouldn't be a young woman anymore.

'I want a delectable girl,' he told the agency, one day. 'Not some over made-up scrubber. I want a mouth watering young woman, with a complexion like a peach. Have you anyone attractive, appealing, appetizing on your books or not?' The woman at the other end of the phone felt her skin crawl. She would certainly warn any of the escorts about how revolting he was and give them the choice of accompanying him or not.

Carole served Mr Grimes a savoury meat pie for lunch followed by a tasty blackberry crumble. She'd listened to his phone call as she'd listened to many others. Mr Grimes barely noticed her because she always wore very plain thick clothing and no make up, with her hair scraped back as unattractively as possible. Carole kept as much distance as she could from this creepy man, but the wages for a student were good and they were helping her pay her way through college.

Neville Grimes enjoyed his meal. The food was much better than his mother cooked and he looked into the kitchen to ask for more. 'That was a nice meal Carole. Any more?'

'Thank you Mr Grimes, I'll bring it through,' she spoke formally.

He looked at her more closely. 'She wouldn't look bad if she had breast implants and her hair bleached. At last I may have found the right woman,' he thought.

'Please call me Neville. Do you know that I'm a very rich man?'

'Yes, Mr Grimes…. Neville. I had gathered that.'

'I could make your life very comfortable. I could buy you anything you want. You'd suit me very well. You can cook and with a bit of work you could be quite attractive. You'd never have to finish your college course or work again. Are you interested?' He knew she'd accept his proposal for he was so rich, she'd be foolish to refuse.

'I'll be back tonight,' she smiled. 'Seven pm. And I'll make an effort with my appearance.'

'Oh no, don't rush off. We could get to know each other.'

'Sorry, but I need the time to get ready. Smarten myself up. After all I know you want a perfect woman.'

Carole evaded his grasp, picked up her coat and slipped her wage packet into a pocket, with the speed of youth, that leaves a fifty five year old bewildered.

'See you at seven,' she called as she descended the steps out of the flat two at a time.

At seven o'clock Neville Grimes was dressed in his whitest shirt and smart trousers with a knife edge crease down the front. This was *his* time. All these years of saving had been worth it.

At seven thirty he tried her mobile but there was no answer. By eight thirty he realized she wasn't coming. Slowly it began to dawn on him that he might not find the perfect woman. There are people that you cannot buy. He settled down to review his investments. At least they gave him pleasure.

There Are No Flowers

The church is large and made of red sandstone that has acquired a dark hue through the years. No amount of heating could make the high vaulted ceilings and brightly coloured windows seem welcoming now. Here I stood as your bride in my gown of thick rustling ivory silk and you stood and made your promises wearing a deep grey suit. Who would have guessed, when we stood side by side all those years ago, how it would end? It certainly wasn't the end you planned.

As Pachelbel's 'Canon' was playing, all our friends and relatives sat waiting patiently for the wedding to start. The smell of white roses and lilies pervaded the church and sunlight streamed through the glass, extending colours like a magical veil.

My father held out his arm as the music changed to 'Here comes the bride' and his eyes glistened with unshed tears. I linked my arm through his and adjusted the lace over my dark hair, I felt his arm shaking. I tried to walk elegantly by his side to where you waited, but everyone was grinning at me and I couldn't help but grin back. I looked at you with love and you smiled, but your eyes quickly moved away again. I know *now* we see only what we want to see and I wanted to see your love.

After the hectic photographs and wedding meal we danced together and you held me in your arms. Life was perfect at that moment. The music touched my soul and I was surrounded by all those special friends and family, who were wishing us happiness.

Although there is a romantic part of me, I was never so naive as to think that such perfection would stay the same, but nothing prepared me for our future. I'll always remember the time I prepared the food for our first guests in our new home. I'd cleaned the house from top to bottom and although it needed decorating everything looked spotless. Then I prepared a special meal, but you weren't pleased.

'You can't serve that mush to other people; for goodness sake, we'll order some take-a-way.'

'What's wrong with it?' I asked but you just picked up the phone and started ordering.

'Clear it away before they come,' you shouted as you went to change.

Soon you were making excuses for friends not to come round and gradually none came. From criticising my cooking you slowly began to take apart everything I did and who I was. If I wore any make-up you called me a slut and gradually I descended into that isolated hell where you ruled. I had no mind, no brain, no willpower and very few friends, but my closest friends Marcia and Angela never gave up. They rang me sometimes when you were at work, but you never knew.

One day I went to meet Marcia and Angela in town. I carefully applied some foundation make up over the bruise on my cheek and wore a long sleeved T-shirt to cover the marks on my arm. The nausea I felt, I put down to worry that you might find out I was seeing my friends. How ridiculous had I become, to think that seeing friends was a sin? I thought I'd be safe, because you'd told me that you were going to London that day and would be late home.

Angela arrived looking stunning in a short red wool dress. She wore matching heels, which were not so high that she tottered. In complete contrast Marcia wore tailored black jeans and a double layered embroidered T shirt, reminiscent of the sixties. She looked beautiful. I felt so dowdy in my plain jeans and T-shirt, but they were so pleased to see me I soon forgot how awful I looked.

We were sitting in the café when in you walked with a young girl. Her hair was deep brown, like mine, and she wore a skirt as short as I used to wear. Luckily you took a seat and you sat with your back to me. My stomach ached with how attentive you were towards her. I moved my chair further back so that I was hidden from you behind a tall plastic pot plant, which was intended to add ambience to the café.

'Mark's just walked in with that girl,' I whispered. 'What am I going to do? He'll kill me if he thinks I'm out wasting money.'

'Listen to yourself girl,' Angela replied, 'You're worried you're in the wrong for seeing your friends. He's here with another woman and from the way he's touching her they're more than just friends. It's time to leave him and get your life back.'

'Yes,' said Marcia, 'Anyone can see you're terrified of him and that's no way to live. Come and stay with me for a while.'

We stayed and ate our meal, because I was too frightened to leave and I threw up in the ladies afterwards. Just before we all said good-bye Marcia popped into the chemists and came out with a pregnancy testing kit.

'This is for you and if you're expecting you must leave. You can go to my parents in Eastbourne if you want to get right away. They're always looking for help with their hotel and there'd be accommodation.'

Later that day I was on the train to Eastbourne with half the money from our savings account. It had been lucky you were saving up to get a sports car or I'm sure all of the money would have gone on alcohol. I had to break the cabinet open to get the account book but something inside me had cracked. Just being with my friends again made me see how much I'd changed and Marcia was right. I couldn't risk you hurting the baby.

Eastbourne was wonderful. Marcia's family welcomed me into the hotel business and it became my home. The hotel was rarely full in those days and they gave me a large room over the laundry. It was a little noisy as the machines ran at night but it was warm and always smelled so fresh. My figure turned from gaunt, to plump and finally the balloon burst and Jenny was born. Jenny brightened the whole world with her happy smile and curiosity. In those first years my help in the hotel was backstage and I just fitted in what I could around her needs but Marcia's parents were great. I cleaned rooms when Jenny slept and later I took her and her toys from room to room and I did the job well because of you. I made the perfect bed because I'd learned if I left a crease it would make you angry. I took on some ironing and Marcia's parents were so grateful that I worked without fuss but they also understood the needs of Jenny, who they grew to love.

By the time Jenny started school, my work changed. I did the wages and the accounts. I worked on reception and helped serve the evening meals when there was a big party. Angela brought her children to stay in Eastbourne often and Marcia frequently visited her parents. Sometimes we all met up together. They were glad to have their old friend back and I stopped being frightened and dowdy.

Did you ever wonder what my parents thought of you? Probably not. Well let me tell you anyway.

On a visit last year my dad asked, 'Did Mark ever catch up with you?'

'No. I did wonder if he'd try when we got divorced but he's never turned up.'

'Never liked the chap. Something about him that didn't ring true but couldn't put my finger on it.'

'Sorry, dad. I've put you and mum through it and caused you loads of worry.'

'Don't be daft. It wasn't your fault but he's probably doing the same to some other poor girl though. These bullies don't give up.'

'Well let's just hope she's stronger than I was.'

Dad and I never spoke of you again.

It was a few months after my visit home, when I was sitting having a cup of tea and reading the newspaper after all the guests had finished their breakfast, that I saw your face again. Your striking good looks stared at me out of the paper and beside your picture was that of a rather plain young girl; a girl with pale skin and a haunted look in her eyes.

'Was it a crime of passion?' the headline screamed out at me. 'Tracy Roberts was arrested yesterday for killing her husband with a bread knife. Neighbours said that they heard the couple rowing almost daily when he returned home from the pub. It is thought that Tracy was being frequently hit by her husband. None of her friends have come forward to put her side of the story.'

I could feel the blood drain from my face and my hands started to shake. It could have been me in Tracy's position. What should I do?

Jenny knew there was something wrong when I picked her up from school. She could tell by my face. We went for a walk in Prince's Park so that we could talk.

'Jenny, your father and I couldn't live together. He was an unhappy man and he was often... well unkind. Today I learned that he died. I'm sorry. I know one day you'd have liked to meet him and now that isn't going to happen.'

Jenny gave me a hug. 'I've never wanted to meet him. You're not to be cross, but Aunty Marcia told me what he was like. I pestered her and pestered her until she did. I really wanted to know about him but once she'd filled me in, I thought 'I'm better off without him.' There's something else, isn't there?'

'Well yes my love. He was murdered by his new wife. I've been wondering if I should speak up for her.'

'Hmmm tricky one that. Well mum, you always say to me to look at the consequences. How will you feel if she gets locked away for years for murder and how will you feel if you speak up for her and she gets off with a light sentence?'

I smiled at my daughter.

So here we are now; the trial is set for August and after my chat with the police, the charges against Tracy were changed to manslaughter, but the funeral is today.

Jenny and I walk up the narrow path to the large oak doorway. There's a much smaller door within the larger one and we climb through. It's still winter and outside. There's frost on the ground but the heating is on high within the building. No amount of heating could make the high vaulted ceilings and brightly coloured windows seem welcoming now.

57

I notice first the lack of flowers. The church is bare of white lilies and roses. There are also few people. My daughter clutches my hand tightly. We sit quietly through the short service where the vicar tries to say nice things about a man he's never met.

I'm surprised that there isn't a group of your drinking friends here, for you always told a good joke and were generous to them. Perhaps your anger slipped over into their lives or are they giving you the perfect send-off at the Pig and Whistle?

Tracy, with the pale haunted face, is sitting in a pew to the left. Beside her is an older suited woman with very short hair. I suspect she's a police officer. Tracy doesn't hold her handkerchief to her eyes, which are blank and glazed. I'd reach out to comfort her but she seems unaware that anyone is here.

'So good-bye Mark; who'd have thought I'd have been sitting here and not you. When you threw me down the stairs and my head bled and you wouldn't call an ambulance. Yet somehow I was still there the next morning and when you put your hands round my throat and squeezed until the world spun before my eyes, I knew I'd die; but again somehow I survived. Now Mark in the silence of my mind I'm here to let you know that you've a beautiful daughter. Maybe if you'd have known, she'd have saved you as she saved me, but I couldn't risk it. You broke me until I was too frightened even to leave, but you gave me Jenny, so I can't hate you now. She was my impetus to go; my way forward to freedom. I've gone from strength to strength, with a job I love and friends who are loyal. Jenny's the greatest gift that anyone's given me, so although there are no flowers, we've come to say, 'Good-bye'.

And strangely, as you're taken from the church, the smell of lilies and roses comes to me, as Jenny and I step out through the wooden door into a crisp, but warming day.

Journey Home

My mother's flat was too hot. The windows wouldn't open because some kind soul had painted the frames shut. I took a deep sigh and weaved my way through the many pieces of dark brown furniture and started to clear away the coffee things. After a few days of being here I was ready to get back to my husband and our clutter free home. Mum liked a bit of company but because she didn't get out much her conversation was mainly about what had happened on the soaps. When it was time to leave she always tried to persuade me to stay and today was no different.

'I know - why don't you stop for lunch?' Mum said. ' We can go to that new place along the beach.'

'Mum don't do this. I have a very long journey and if I get caught in traffic on the motorway, it's murder.'

'It's just that I don't see you very often and while you're here, well it's lovely.'

'That's emotional blackmail and you know it,' I smiled. You couldn't help but love her. People thought that she had a touch of dementia, but she'd always been a little different. When she was younger she claimed she could see into the future. Nobody believed her of course, but once or twice she was right with her predictions. Dad said that if you predict enough things eventually one or two will be right. Mum doesn't do that anymore, but she does make it hard to leave her.

'I wonder if you could change the light bulb in the bathroom before you go. It's just a little too high for me to reach.'

I went and collected a bulb from the kitchen cupboard. The bulb was changed in five minutes. Her next ploy would be she'd lost something.

'Aaaaaaggggghhhh,' she screamed. I rushed over to her. 'The pain is dreadful,' she whispered. 'Please don't leave me.'

Picking up the phone I said quietly, 'It'll be all right, Mum. I'm calling an ambulance. Don't worry. I'll stay.'

Suddenly the phone was grabbed. 'Don't do that. I'm fine now. The pain's gone.'

'Mum what are you playing at? I know you don't like me leaving, but you know I have to go. You don't usually play tricks like that. I was really worried.'

'I'm sorry. It's just...' she started to say.

'Look here's my mobile phone number. If you can't get me at home you can ring this number and I'll be there and if I can't answer it, I'll call back as soon as I can.'

I gave her a big hug and she said, 'Give Daddy my love.' As my Dad had died ten years ago I realized that maybe Mum was getting a bit confused. Rose, who had the flat next door, came to sit with Mum, so I could leave, but Mum might need to come and live with us in the near future. It was something to think about.

The traffic was heavy with cars and lorries by the time I hit the M25. I knew I just had to keep going. There was the M1 and the M6 still to do. It was always such a long journey that I listened to music which helped it to pass. As I walked through the front door, relieved to be home, I realized I couldn't remember all of the journey. I often find that these days.

'Bertie, I'm home,' I called. Unusually there was no reply. I could hear him in the bathroom. The news was blaring out from the television so I plonked myself down on the sofa to watch it for five minutes and then I'd make us both a nice cup of tea.

The newsreader was saying, 'There was a seven car pile up on the M1, which is causing long delays. The vehicles are being removed but there are now tailbacks in both directions. One person was killed in the accident. Gemma Daniels a 62 year old woman from Manchester died before the ambulance reached her. The police think she may have been distracted by her mobile phone ringing, although it is not thought she was using her phone as it was still in her handbag. Her family have been informed.'

I was shocked. I'd been on that very road today. I must have just missed it and fancy the victim having the same name as me. I must tell Bertie. I walked towards the bathroom as the door opened. I started to speak to him, but Bertie's skin was pale, almost grey and his eyes were bloodshot as if he'd been crying. What on earth had happened while I'd been away?

And then he walked right through me.

The House

Samantha used the large metal key to let herself into the house. It was her fiancé's house, left to him by his parents, who'd been killed in an accident. She shivered and switched on the lights, even though outside there would be hours of daylight left.

The rooms were all large and regular with high ceilings and the furnishings were supposedly homely, but Sam felt the atmosphere was not good. It was as if the house didn't want her here. She could almost feel another presence and it was not a friendly one and yet when Rob was with her everything was fine.

'This is ridiculous,' she said to herself and marched towards the kitchen with her bags of shopping. She switched the radio on to some loud music and set about preparing the evening meal. As she was chopping onions and taking the skins off large juicy tomatoes, strange thoughts kept coming into her head.

'Get out while you can. Run for your life. Don't stay.'

Sam turned the music up and boiled some water for the pasta. Rob would be home at any minute. As he walked through the kitchen door five minutes later she breathed a sigh of relief. She couldn't believe they were getting married. The sight of him made her feel so alive. He strode over to where she was standing, turning the radio off as he passed, and pulled her towards him.

'How's my beautiful girl today?'

Ordinarily Sam would have found such a remark patronizing, but love turns everything upside down and she answered, 'Fine, you had a good day?'

'Not too bad. Look I know you can't annoy any neighbours here because we're miles away from them, but did you need to have the music so loud? People will think you're mad.'

Sam refrained from saying that there were no people to hear. There was no point in having an argument.

'It's just when you're not here it's a bit quiet and …oh, never mind. Dinner will be five minutes,' she said as she stirred the sauce.

'It's not out of a tin is it?'

Sam smiled, 'No, it's all freshly cooked, just as you like it.'

After dinner they settled down to sorting out the final wedding arrangements. As the evening went on Sam could hear a strange voice in her head.

'Don't do it!' it said and this was followed shortly by. 'You're in danger'

Hearing voices isn't exactly normal so Sam kept the warnings to herself. She didn't want to do anything to put him off, so she smiled through her unease, while quietly wondering if she was going insane.

Samantha had a late start the following day and when she woke the sun was shining through the bedroom window. There was no sign of Rob, so he obviously had left to go to work. She reached over to look at her watch and saw a piece of paper on the bedside cabinet.

'No doubt Rob had left her a little love note; he was very romantic,' she thought, but as she examined both sides of the paper she realized it was completely blank.

'Never mind. He probably had been going to leave a note but then ran out of time.'

She stretched and relaxed thinking about how lucky she was to be marrying her dream man. One or two of her friends had tried to put the dampener on things, pointing out that she hardly knew him; they were probably jealous. She ignored them because no-one had ever made her feel as he did. His tall frame made her feel protected. You could sink into his brown eyes. They were so mesmerising and he had the blackest hair with a raven's sheen.

Sam was brought back to reality by the house creaking. The windows rattled like someone chattering, but in the warmth of the bed Sam felt safe. She snuggled down wondering why Rob should be interested in her with her mousy hair and funny little pixie face. Her musings were interrupted by her mobile ringing.

'You up yet or you'll be late for your appointment.'

'Yes, Mr Jameson,' she replied laughing, throwing back the covers. 'I'm getting up now.'

The coldness of the room hit her and she grabbed her thick dressing gown and headed for the bathroom. Soon she was showered and dressed and ready to go to the doctor's appointment for a check up. They had decided to make sure they were both healthy before the marriage and check that they could have children. It was Rob's idea really but as things had turned out she was more than happy to go along with it.

She took her coffee back into the bedroom and balanced it on the bedside cabinet while she rummaged through her bag for some make-up. Suddenly the cup crashed to the floor, spilling the coffee on the carpet. Sam ran to the kitchen.

'It mustn't stain.' She thought because if there was one thing that annoyed Rob it was mess. Quickly she picked up a bowl of soapy water and a floor cloth and took it back to the bedroom.

'Phew how lucky was that,' she thought. 'Most of the coffee has fallen onto the blank notepaper which was also on the floor.'

She cleaned the carpet until it was immaculate and then realized how late it was getting. Rushing into the kitchen she went to throw away the paper in the bin but as she did so, she saw there was writing on the paper.

You are in danger. Leave now and don't come back.
P.J.

As she stood there looking at the message it faded before her eyes. Sam grabbed her bag and ran out of the house. Her heart was racing and she felt as if she had thunder in her ears. When she reached the safety of her car she paused.

What should she do and who was P.J.?

The question was answered purely by chance when she returned to the house later in the day. She'd left coming back as late as she could because she didn't want to spend too much time there without Rob, and the phone was ringing as she opened the door.

'Hello, may I ask, who am I speaking to?'

'It's Samantha Saunders, Rob's fiancée.'

'My name is Amanda. I'm Pauline's sister. I don't suppose you know where I can get hold of her. I didn't even know they'd got divorced.'

'Who's got divorced?' Sam asked.

'Why Rob and Pauline of course. I haven't heard from her for ages. Look I'll leave my number. I know Rob won't want to speak to me 'cos, we didn't get on, but I just want to contact my sister.'

'Pauline Jameson,' Sam thought. 'P.J. and I didn't even know he'd been married.'

Sam took the number down and put it in her bag. She refreshed her make up as her mind went through a hundred improbable reasons about why Rob had not mentioned his former wife. She looked up just as Rob walked through the door.

'You ready?' he asked.

'Yes, let's go.' Sam replied. She didn't mention the phone call because she needed time to think and time was short as they'd agreed to dine out with one of Rob's important clients.

The following day Rob was off to America on business. It was to be his last trip before the wedding. Sam got up and had breakfast with him and promised she'd be at the house next week when he got back.

* * * * * *

Pauline felt no jealously when she saw her handsome husband bring back the pixie faced girl with slightly slanting eyes. She recognised the bedazzled look of a young girl in love and although Pauline was trapped in this house she couldn't sit around and do nothing. She almost smiled to herself because she couldn't actually sit.

She tried to make the house unwelcoming and was quite pleased with the effect until Rob came home from work. Sam as she later gathered her name to be, was so besotted that she was not listening to all the warnings she was being given.

Pauline had tried screaming at the top of her voice.

'Get out while you can. Don't stop here. Don't stay.' It had taken a lot of energy but had caused hardly any response from Sam.

She'd tried banging on the windows but it had no effect. If only she was more skilled.

It was when she'd written the note and managed to knock coffee over it, that she knew her message was beginning to get across, but would she be too late?

She went to the bookcase and took out the smallest book and tore out a blank page. She wrote on it in thick black ink, which somehow disappeared as it was passed over to the live world. Pauline decided to tell Sam exactly what had happened so she knew how much danger there was.

* * * * * *

Sam downed a cup of coffee before leaving the house. There were so many unanswered questions, not least why she didn't trust Rob enough to tell him that she knew about his marriage. Then she noticed the piece of paper by her cup. Examining it closely she saw there were no words, but remembered the invisible ink trick from yesterday. She held the note over the sink and poured the remainder of her coffee over it.

***Rob killed me. I am under the dining room
floor. You must get away.***
   P.J.

As before the words disappeared while she
watched. Samantha wondered what she should do.
Was this some cruel joke someone was playing on her
and was she prepared to give up the wonderful future
they'd planned?

'I need evidence,' she thought.

She took a deep breath and went into the
dining room. It all looked so normal, but she had to
know the truth. She crawled under the table to
examine the carpet but it looked fine. The wind blew
down the chimney and the old sash windows rattled.
She remembered that Rob had never told her about
P.J. She moved the chairs and then dragged the table
to one side and started to roll back the carpet. She
could feel the adrenaline pumping round her body and
it gave her the strength to manoeuvre back the carpet.
As the unvarnished floorboards became visible she
noticed two things. The first was there was a muddy
brown stain on the back of the carpet and the second
was that there were some bright new nails on some of
the floorboards. They stood out because the rest were
black.

Not bothering to put the carpet back she ran
from the house and went straight to the police station.
She told Inspector Scott her story about a missing
wife, who her fiancé had never mentioned and the
stain on the back of the carpet and the new nails. As
she was speaking she expected him to tell her to go
away. She knew she sounded slightly hysterical and
thought he must think her completely round the bend.

Instead he smiled, 'So are you inviting us to the house to take a look, Miss Saunders?' as he was gathering his coat, keys and evidence bag.

'Yes Inspector Scott. I am.' And as she said those words she knew she would never marry Rob. Her friends had been right. She didn't know him and worse she didn't trust him.

As they travelled in the car Inspector Scott asked, 'What made you look under the carpet?'

Sam thought quickly knowing that she couldn't say she'd received an invisible message, which she'd read by pouring coffee over it and now didn't have, so she said the first thing that came into her head.

'I thought I'd spring clean before the wedding, while Rob was away.' As she spoke she realized that there wouldn't be any cleaning materials out so she hurriedly added, 'I was preparing the room so I could start the cleaning after I'd run some errands.'

Inspector Scott gave her a wry smile. 'No matter.'

Much later that day, the police found not one but three bodies beneath the floorboards.

'Who can the other's be?' asked Sam.

'So you're sure one of them is his wife?' D.I. Scott asked.

'Well not a hundred per cent perhaps, but she is missing, so it would be logical.'

'On that same basis I suspect that the other two bodies will be that of his parents. He claimed that they went missing at sea after a sailing accident. Perhaps I should explain that I was friends with his old man. Didn't get to know the family much, but his father was frightened of Rob, towards the end. He said they made the place untidy and kept messing up his life. I never believed the sailing accident but had no evidence you see, until today when you invited me in. Be good if you could make the lads some coffee, if you wouldn't mind.'

The 'lads' included at least two women although it was difficult to tell them apart with their papery suits and masks on.

Sam was relieved to get away to the kitchen. She saw the piece of paper by the kettle and quickly made the drinks. She tipped some coffee over the paper and read:

I was trapped here but I can go now. Thank you. Be safe.
P.J.

'Thank *you* P.J.' she whispered and the windows rattled.

* * * * * *

Two months later, when the police had finished all their investigations Sam decided to attend Pauline's funeral in the little village of Netherknot. The chief mourner was Amanda who told Sam how much Pauline had wanted a baby.

'It turned out that Pauline couldn't have children. She was so obsessive about having a baby we had a row and lost touch. I just thought she'd taken off somewhere or he'd kicked her out. Never would've believed he'd have done what he has. ...but there was always something cold about him.....'

As Amanda spoke the music in the church faded and her voice became distant. For a moment Sam was back in the house, looking into those deep brown eyes and then she started to pray, with every part of her being that the life within her, wouldn't be tainted by his father's wickedness.

Secrets and Lies

Sometimes it's only when someone dies that the truth about their life emerges. When Granddad died, secrets that had been hidden for years, came tumbling out. I never could have guessed that the jigsaw of his life would turn mine upside down.

Granddad lived on his own, in the house he'd shared with my grandmother, just round the corner from Mum and me. We both visited often. He was always up to something, such as planting seeds, building bird boxes, mending a toy for a neighbour's child and he used to tell stories of people he'd met on the bus or in the park. Whatever you did, he never judged you and whoever you brought round he would always welcome them. Quite simply I loved him.

I'd just started dating Paul. He was an artist and earned virtually nothing, but he'd do anything for anyone. Mum felt that as Paul was around she'd like to go off and visit my sister, Ellen and her family, in Australia. She didn't need to worry about me because at twenty I was perfectly capable of looking after myself.

Granddad said Paul and I were like two mahogany bookends, both tall and thin with rich brown hair, although Paul was a good six inches taller. The only difference he noticed was our eyes. Mine were a deep sea green and Paul's were the brightest hypnotic blue.

Mum had just arrived in Australia when Granddad died. It was the summer of 1993. She returned immediately. After the funeral I told her to go back; Mum deserved time with Ellen and the children. A few days later Paul came round to help me sort out Granddad's house.

'I'm going to sort through his desk and then the books. Perhaps you can sort his clothes. Bag them up for the charity shop, but throw away anything too worn.'

Paul hugged me and then we started working. After several hours I heard Paul clunking down the stairs.

'I remember you buying this scarf for him for his birthday last year. Here, you should keep it.'

I wrapped it round my neck and it felt comforting.

'I'm going out to get us some sandwiches. Back in half an hour,' he said.

The house was quiet. I remembered the sounds of Granddad's footsteps on the stone kitchen floor and his gentle voice. I remembered him listening to his favourite radio four programme, 'Morning Story'. Twice he'd read his own stories on the programme and he'd enjoyed listening to the work of others. There was no sound now except for the noise I made turning over papers.

I stood up, stretched and went to the bookcase. The books were stuffed in at any angle and varied in both height and size. The top shelf had his own books that he'd written over the decades and on that shelf all the books stood upright, like soldiers on guard. They were a lasting tribute to the humorous and ironic observations he made about life. Out of the medley on the lower shelves I took out a number of books and browsed. As I flipped through pages, discovering old friends I'd love to revisit, and intriguing extracts of ones I'd never seen, I came across a little green bound book named 'The

Complete Sherlock Homes' by Arthur Conan Doyle. Dust coated it. I remembered reading those stories as a young teenager and hadn't even known Granddad had a copy. As I opened the cover a small press cutting, browned with age, fell on the floor. I began to read it and my heart started thumping. It couldn't be true. My Granddad couldn't have done that. I read it again slowly just to check if I'd understood.

Killer used Kitchen Knife

Thomas Mullens (21) was found guilty of manslaughter today in the Crown Court at Chester. He killed his former classmate with a kitchen knife on the 26th April 1934. The victim, Alfred Butcher was also 21 years old.

Mullens said that Butcher was attacking him and he picked up the knife without thinking. He had no intention of killing Butcher. The police stated that the defendant had been extremely upset when they arrived. The judge said he had taken into account that Mullens had called the police himself and waited for their arrival.

Mullens pleaded guilty and was given a seven year sentence. The medical reports showed that Mullens was not a man of a violent disposition and his action had been out of character. Mullens had no previous record.

His girlfriend Betty Swan said 'I will stand by Thomas. He is a good man and this was a terrible mistake.'

How would I tell Mum? I thought I was going to faint and sat down quickly. The silence echoed around me.

When Paul came back and found me so distressed he suggested we went out to the park for some fresh air. As we walked along the graveled paths, vibrant coloured flowers blurred into random patterns through my tears, like a moving kaleidoscope.

Paul's gentle voice broke into my thoughts. 'Throw the cutting away Lynne. It was a long time ago and you need to leave it in the past.'

I felt much better being outside. The sun warmed my skin and a gentle breeze brushed my cheeks. I knew Paul's words were wise and I valued his opinion but I just needed to know the truth. Nothing else mattered.

The following day I went back to the house alone and found the telephone number of Bert, one of Granddad's oldest friends, and I arranged to meet him in the pub on Saturday.

When I pushed open the pub door Bert was sitting in the corner of the Rose and Crown waiting for me.

'Hello Lynne, I've been looking forward to this date with a pretty girl all week.' He smiled. 'Let me get you a drink.'

'Thank you, a glass of coke would be lovely.'

When he returned he patiently answered my questions.

'From the photographs I've seen, you went to school with Granddad.'

'That's right.'

'I've been sorting out his house for Mum and as I looked at a book this clipping fell out.' I placed it on the table. 'I just can't believe it's true. I would really like to know anything you can tell me.'

Bert looked at the cutting with sadness, but it was obviously no surprise to him.

'I know he pleaded guilty and spent a few years in prison just before the war. Tom never really spoke about it. All I can tell you is that I never believed he was capable of it. He was going out with Betty Swan at the time. She didn't have a good reputation, in the days when reputation mattered, but Tom never paid any heed to what people said.'

'What about Alf Butcher? What can you tell me about him?'

'Well Alf was a bit of a nightmare. He was always after the girls and quite successful, if you know what I mean. As often as not he would be drunk in the evenings and it was not unheard of for him to be in a punch up on a Saturday night. I never liked him much.'

'Did Granddad *never* talk about what happened?'

'No, he didn't want to and I never pushed it, but I will say that in all the years I knew him I never saw him lose his temper and if trouble was brewing, it would always be your grandfather who calmed everything down. He was a lovely man and he loved your grandmother and your mum. He was always talking about you and your sister, he was.'

'I do miss him, so much. It's lovely to just talk about him.'

'Well I miss him too. You know the important thing is, that if he did something so very wrong, he spent the rest of his life doing good and maybe there's another explanation that we'll never know.

One thing I'm sure of is he wouldn't want you fretting about it all.'

'Thanks Bert.'

Although I kept in touch with Mum and explained all I was doing, I thought she was too far away to be given this awful news. Paul had an exhibition to prepare for and was working hard to get his pictures ready for the following week so I went back to the house alone. I'd arranged for a charity to come and pick up some of the solid bits of furniture, which they could use for people being re-housed. Afterwards I climbed up to the attic to clear it out. It was full of boxes crammed with books, magazines and items no longer used. The sunlight streamed in through the skylight showing dancing dust particles as I moved things around. It was then I found the box of diaries. Granddad always kept a diary. He said it helped him with ideas for characters for his books. I would take them home to read properly but as I sat on the floor I searched for the one dated 1934. There it was. I flicked open the page to the date mentioned in the cutting.

26 April 1934

What a terrible day! Betty called to say that Alf had attacked her. She'd told him she was going out with me but he'd had a drink and wouldn't take no for an answer.

She'd tried to run away but the back door was shut. He'd caught up with her in the kitchen and lunged at her. In desperation she'd picked up a knife and stuck it in him. She was hysterical. I had no idea what to do to help.

I went round to hers and Alf was slumped on the floor. He had no pulse. I wiped her prints off the knife and handled it myself. We agreed it'd be best for me to say I'd done it. I couldn't bear the thought of her going to jail. She hugged me and I got covered in Alf's blood. It was horrid.

While I called the police she cleaned herself up and changed her clothes. I hope I've done the right thing.

He was innocent. How could that woman let him take responsibility for her crime? Betty Swan was her name and I intended to find her. With foolhardy enthusiasm I went to St Catherine's house near Waterloo and found that Betty Swan had married a man called William Walsh. More research through telephone directories and a number of calls revealed that Mrs. Walsh was now in a nursing home in Chester. I telephoned and made an appointment to see her the next day.

Betty Walsh seemed a frail woman huddled in her large armchair under a thick blanket. She smiled vaguely at me until she realized that I wanted her to confirm her part on that dreadful day.

Then she whispered, 'I will never do as you ask. I don't want to face my children with that information.' I was just about to try to persuade her when she screamed, 'GET OUT. GO AWAY'. The carer in charge came quickly and escorted me out, telling me not to return and upset her residents.

I couldn't stop myself from shaking when I went back to the house. I sat in one of the few remaining chairs hugging a mug of tea for warmth, but in the quiet there I realized Paul had been right. It was all in the past and I should have left it alone. My Granddad had made his choices in his life. Who did I think I was that I could sort out such a situation? The only thing that really mattered is that he had been innocent and if anyone found out his dreadful secret I could show them the diary entry. If Granddad had made such a sacrifice for Betty, why should I make her last years miserable?

It was time to get back to my life and celebrate Paul's success in his art exhibition. The diaries were a revelation. Strangely I could hear Granddad's voice when I read them and my heart ached for the torment he observed in prison. It seems he really did have a knack of calming potentially violent situations as there were several accounts of him diverting attention to prevent trouble. My Granddad's secret never quite left me, but I consciously put it to the back of my mind, however three years later it was jolted to the front, when I received a letter from Betty. It was dated just a few days after my visit to her.

3rd October 1993

Dear Lynne,

If you are reading this letter then I've passed away. I thought long and hard after you visited me and decided that for history's sake Thomas's name should be cleared.

As I remember what happened on the night of 26 April 1934 I still shudder with the horror of it. If I am to be honest I was flirting with Alf, but not with the intention of it going anywhere. It was exciting to have two young men in love with me. Possibly you can't imagine it, but in my younger days I was considered attractive. Old age makes us all look alike; pale reflections of our youth.

Anyway Alf made a pass at me and when I said no, we fought. I got away from him but not far. By that time I was really scared. I stabbed Alf with the knife before I'd realized what I was doing. It was so quick.

Your grandfather sorted it all out and took the blame. Of course I should have waited for him but I was young. After a year I wrote to him and said we were not a couple anymore. He agreed and said whatever it was we'd had didn't exist any longer. What I didn't tell him was I already had married William and had my first child, Rose. Thomas probably knew that Rose was his daughter when he found out about her but he kept quiet about it. William always treated Rose as his own. I have left her a letter so that she will know the truth by now.

Thomas was released early because of his good behaviour, so he only served five years. Perhaps that seems a long time to you, but he had his writing. His first book used a lot of the experiences he had while in prison.
Don't judge me too harshly, Lynne. Your grandfather never did.
Yours truly
Betty Walsh

I placed the letter and the press cutting inside the 1934 diary. It was time to tell Mum her father's story. Tears ran down her face as she realized what her father had suffered and later we agreed that I should write it all down so that there was a record for the future, so here it is. One day I will apply for a pardon for Granddad from the Home Secretary, but right now I'm just getting my head round the fact I've got another aunt - if what Betty has written is the truth.

Time's Marching

Sally brushed her hair until it shone and added a touch of pale lipstick to her lips. She didn't really 'do' make up, as there were so many more interesting things to do in the world; like seeing her boyfriend or riding her horse, Sundance.

She took a deep breath and went downstairs, where her mother, Diana, was waiting to take her out. This ritual had gone on for the last six years, since she was twelve. Sally thought the time for these formal visits needed to come to an end. She didn't enjoy the disapproving looks her mother gave her and she was fairly sure her mother didn't want to see her anyway.

'Hello Mother,' she greeted her with a peck on the cheek.

'Hello darling. Well let me look at you. You're looking …um healthy. Let's go shopping and see if we can't smarten you up a bit.'

'I'd rather go to Chester Zoo,' said Sally.

'Nonsense, every girl likes buying clothes.'

'I don't,' thought Sally, but there was no point in saying anything. Her father, Max, made a grimace at her as they left the house.

Diana drove too fast and then abandoned the car across two car parking spaces in the multi-storey car park. They went down in the lift and Diana tottered over the road to a smart restaurant that had live lobsters, which you could sentence to death and eat for your meal. Sally felt faintly queasy looking at the poor creatures, but luckily her mother was on one of her diets so the lobsters were at least safe for the time being.

'Now darling,' her mother said when they had sat down, 'we need to have a serious talk. You've been brought up by a man, bless him, and he's done his best, but you need your mother to sort you out. You're looking a little dowdy and there's so much that can be done these days.

'Mother, I look like I look. I don't care.'

'Darling, don't talk rubbish. How will you find a nice young man if you don't make the effort? All we need to do is to have you teeth straightened and whitened and get your hair a decent cut and maybe dyed. Perhaps you could have a small boob job to make yourself look a bit more womanly and then you'd be amazed by what some well cut clothes would do for you.'

'No. I am eighteen and I can do what I like...' started Sally.

'I know it's great isn't it? Your father can't stop you improving yourself now.'

The waiter appeared with sandwiches and juice for Sally and salad and a mineral water for Diana. Diana waved him away as he finished placing the food in front of them.

'Thank you,' said Sally looking apologetically to the waiter. 'Now mother, you need to listen. I am not your age and I don't have to try to look young. I am young. I don't have to dress up, because I work on a farm and my hobby is horse riding. I understand you mean well, but I am not you and don't want to be you.'

'But darling, how will you attract a man?'

'Well strange as it may seem to you, I have managed to find one or two boyfriends so far and I have no intention of settling down in the near future.

Here look at my proms picture.' Sally pressed some buttons on her phone and handed it over to Diana.

'You look very pretty dear but I could make you beautiful. Wouldn't you like to look like me? Why if you had a few nips and tucks in a couple of years, you would look young through your thirties and forties, and a little Botox on your lips now would just make you look more desirable.'

Sally picked up her phone again and found another photo. 'What do you think of him?'

Diana peered at the phone. 'Oh he's good looking. Who's he?'

'Jason's my boyfriend and he likes me as I am.'

'But that's my point darling. You won't stay as you are. Time will steal that smooth skin and paint it with ugly wrinkles and your face will turn into a blancmange and fall to the floor. We need to take action now.'

'Time will paint Jason's face with laughter lines and he'll probably put on a bit of weight and lose a bit of hair. Maybe I'll be with him and maybe I won't. Who knows?'

'But wouldn't you like to look like me at my age?' Diana asked.

'I think nature blessed you with beauty mother, but look at Gran; she's beautiful too and she has just let time enhance her face. That's what I'm going to do too.'

'Well really. I was just trying to help. I don't know how you can compare your Gran to me.' Diana left the untouched salad on the plate and walked out.

Sally finished her sandwiches in silence. 'It was unfair to compare Gran to mother. Gran was softly rounded and always there. She had a light sense of humour and her house was always busy with people eating cake or stopping over. Her mother was always needy and lonely, in her expensive clothes and too tight face. Her wide fat lips looked out of place in the mask like face.' Suddenly Sally understood what she had to do. She threw down enough notes to pay the bill and ran out of the restaurant to the car park. Her mother was just getting into the car.

'I really want to spend some time with you, mum, but not shopping or being improved. Let's go to Gran's house for a cup of tea and catch up on each other's lives. You're right; time is marching on for all of us, so let's not leave each other on bad terms.'

'You know very well Gran doesn't approve of me and always looks at me critically.'

Sally smiled, 'And you know very well Gran loves you to bits and misses you – so come on.'

Her mother paused and then smiled. She threw the keys to Sally. 'You drive,' she said as she took off her designer jacket, sat down in the car and slipped the stilettos off her feet.

***

As Sally eased the car into her Gran's drive she breathed a sigh of relief. She'd driven it without hitting anything. The steering was much more sensitive than the old Landrover she was used to driving.

She popped her head round her Gran's door and saw Percy and her Gran sitting at the kitchen table with a large chocolate cake and a pot of tea. Percy was a local gardener, who was an old family friend. He was tall with pure white hair and twinkly eyes.

'Hi Gran, I've brought a visitor for you. Hope that's ok.'

Diana now reunited with her heels and having replenished her lipstick swept into the kitchen and went over to Gran.

'Hello mother, how are you?'

Gran paused and took a good look at Diana. Then in her usual welcoming manner she kissed her daughter. Diana straightened up and smoothed down her skirt.

'Come on in,' said Gran. 'I'll make a fresh pot of tea. Diana do you remember Percy?'

'Of course I do. I never forget a good looking man.'

'Mother!' Sally said in a slightly shocked voice as Percy looked over to Gran.

'Well I must be off,' said Percy. 'I've a lawn to mow before the rain sets in.'

'Please don't go because of us. If you stay my mother will be polite to me. As soon as you leave she'll start nagging,' said Diana with a winning smile.

'I don't nag,' said Gran firmly, 'and as I haven't seen you for years I'm not likely to start now. Percy you know you're always welcome here and you haven't finished your cake.' Gran placed some more cups, saucers and plates on the table.

Sally started cutting a slice of the dark brown sponge. 'Cake mum?'

'No, thank you. That'll be about 500 calories. You'd probably have to do a twenty mile walk to compensate.'

'Yes, but you haven't tried it. It's delicious,' said Sally tucking in to the creamy icing. Percy visibly relaxed and picked up his cake.

'So what have you been doing with yourself, Diana? I can see some of the things,' she said pointedly looking at Diana's lips.

'I knew this was a mistake. You've always disapproved of me.'

'I don't disapprove of you. I just wish you could be happy. Are you happy?'

'Well I have been,' replied Diana. 'I married this marvellous man. He had a house in the States and a yacht. We went travelling all the time and met so many people.'

'That sounds fun,' said Gran.

'Then he left. He found a younger woman. Said she was more fun. Still he's having to pay me a packet to get a divorce.' She smiled.

'Well that seems to be making you happy,' said Gran, but there was a note of disapproval in her voice. Sally was surprised how her Gran seemed to change with her mother in the room. Gran never criticized. She just guided.

'Oh come on. If you had the offer of thirty grand a year, you'd say no, would you?'

Nobody spoke and then Percy broke the uncomfortable silence.

'Well it seems to me that you can now afford to settle down and do something you enjoy. Perhaps if you enjoy travelling you should buy a camper van.'

'A camper van, why how sweet. And would you come with me on my travels, Percy?' Diana literally fluttered her eyelashes and Sally cringed inwardly.

Gran and Sally both opened their mouths to say something but Percy was quicker.

'Well child, I just might. As long as I was in the camper van behind yours and was with your mum. You see I've been trying to ask her to marry me for several years.'

All eyes turned to Gran, whose face lit up with a huge smile. 'Well the answer's yes,' she said. 'And I love the idea of going travelling in a camper van.' She was certainly the most beautiful woman in the room at that moment.

Sally kissed her Gran and Percy and wished them happiness. Diana offered her congratulations.

'Well Sally and I will leave you happy lovebirds. Come on Sally, I'll take you home.'

In the car Diana drove quickly and expertly, but Sally noticed a tear slip down her face.

'Why are you crying, Mother?'

'Even your Gran has a happy future ahead of her. I tried so hard to make my marriage work. I'm just a joke.'

'Of course you're not. You're a beautiful and talented lady, but happiness comes from being content with what life offers. It's not about what you look like. One of the things that makes me happy is riding Sundance; being out in the fresh air and feeling the wind in my hair; watching the different seasons as they come and go. You used to ride. Didn't you enjoy it?

'Well I suppose I did a bit.'

'Dad'll lend you his horse and I'll kit you out. Let's go for a ride now.'

They pulled up outside Sally's home. Diana leaned forward and kissed her daughter. 'No, my darling daughter, but I will go home and give some serious thought as to what makes me happy. Of course the one thing I know without thinking is I love seeing you. Perhaps if I move a little closer you could pop in to see me, like you do your Gran.'

'Well, if you provide chocolate cake - it can be boughtcake,' Sally said with a grin, 'it's a deal.'

The Daffodils Bloomed

Ethel lay in her bed and stretched her hand towards her glasses. They were just out of reach. Never mind, she didn't really need them. She could see a blur of yellow out of the window and could pretend that the daffodils, which still danced about in the wind, were at their best, although logic told her they must have bloomed and died by now. They would be waving withered wrinkled heads; a bit like her. She didn't call the nurses to get her glasses because they were so busy and she didn't want to be a nuisance.

Her mind slipped back to the first daffodils that Mark had brought her.

'They're lovely, but for the future, because I'm rather hoping we'll have one, I'd rather see the daffodils in the garden,' she'd said.

He'd smiled. 'That's what I love about you. You're so straightforward and honest. Some women would just have said thank you, but you come right out and say you prefer flowers growing in the ground.'

Well they'd had their future. Mark had brought her a bowl of miniature daffodils for their first anniversary and each year they'd planted more, looking out for different varieties; some pure white and others reminded her of fried eggs. They were all beautiful. Along the way they'd had two wonderful sons, Robin and Charlie. She knew they would be visiting her today. They were good boys.

She remembered when Robin had brought home Claire. How well they'd been suited, both having staid, sensible jobs with good pensions. Now they were saving for their children's future. Robin always phoned her on a Thursday evening and visited every Saturday afternoon. It was Saturday today. She thought of his life like a clock, where routine was used to help space out the years. They would holiday in August, spend Christmas with Claire's parents and New Year with her. Night followed day and for that little family, life was predictable.

His brother Charlie, she thought of like a firework. He was always travelling and ran his own business. He sparkled and dived and exploded and fizzled. He had one daughter from a fleeting relationship; one of the sparkling moments. Charlie had flown in from Spain yesterday, so that he could see her today.

Suddenly Ethel was tired. Life was so busy these days. It wasn't the same since Mark passed away. She still loved her children of course, but they led their own lives. Her friends had been supportive and rarely a day passed without her seeing someone. Even here, where she didn't want to be, people popped in and did her crossword for her, but there was no-one who was just hers. No-one to talk to about shared times or to plan the future with. No-one even to hug. How she'd longed for Mark's warmth, but eventually she'd become used to his empty chair. His dressing gown still hung on the bedroom door at home, so that she could pretend he'd just gone away for a few days, but it had been eight years. Eight long years.

Ethel sighed and her mind wandered back to her childhood, when life had been a struggle but she remembered all the freedom that she and her sister had enjoyed. The things the two of them had got up to were quite frightening. They'd run across the railway line and scrumped apples from the orchard. A grumpy old man shouted at them but they'd both been able to run like the wind. Just as well her grandchildren didn't behave so badly. Then she was back in their old kitchen and she could smell bread baking in the blackened stove and her mother was calling them. The aroma came back to tease her.

'Get your hands washed you scallywags and come and sit up quickly.' There was bread with home-made strawberry jam and a cup of milk for their tea.

Through her failing eyes Ethel could see a bright yellow haze and caught the scent of such freshness. She wished her sons would come soon. If they didn't get to see her she felt sure they'd be upset and she loved them too much to cause them pain.

In the distance she could hear talking. It was hard to make out what they were saying, but she felt a kiss brush her cheek and then recognised Robin's voice.

'Hi Mum, we're both here. I've bought you a bowl of tiny daffodils. Can you smell them?'

Ethel smiled and squeezed his hand. He was such a thoughtful boy. Then big strong arms went round her and she was being cradled in Charlie's arms.

'Love you,' he said. He always knew what to say.

'Love you both,' she managed as the perfume of the daffodils and their golden glow took her away to be with her beloved Mark.

Broken Heart

Sam woke up with her head throbbing. Her mouth was dry and she looked around the unfamiliar room. Her hand felt across the bed for Rob, but he wasn't there. Sam stumbled out of the bed feeling slightly dizzy. She poured cold water from the kettle into a mug and gulped it down, and pushed open the bathroom door, but the room was empty. Where was Rob? His overnight bag was still in the room, but why wasn't he here? It was still early and Rob wasn't a person who got up early.

Something was wrong. Sam could sense it. She drank more water and headed for the shower. When dressed, she tried his mobile, but there was no reply. She ordered some breakfast to be sent up to the hotel room. At least she didn't need to worry about money anymore. She could afford room service, but there had been a time when she'd never have considered using it.

After breakfast her head felt a little less muzzy so she called her best friend, Gemma.

'What shall I do? Rob's nowhere around and I can't contact him, 'cos he's not answering his mobile. I don't know whether to hang on here, or go home.'

'I'd go home. Wherever he's got to, he should have left you a note, even if he just popped out. I suppose he hasn't given you his address yet.'

'No, he's going to take me there next week for the weekend. He said he'll have finished decorating it by then.'

'Well pack everything up and go home. He knows where you are and I'm sure there'll be a simple explanation – like his wife called,' said Gemma.

'Oh don't be like that. He's not married. How could he take me home for the weekend if he had a wife?'

When Sam put the phone down, she packed their things, paid the bill for the hotel and made her way home.

***

At the other side of the city Annabel Eastwood was being attended by her doctor.

'I've given you a sedative, which will make you sleep for a couple of hours. You do need to rest in your condition. When you wake up, the police will need to have a chat to you about last night, but try not to think about it for the moment. Mrs. Jameson, from next door is going to stay over so there's no need to worry. You won't be on your own.'

'Thank you, Doctor Holt.'

The police had cordoned off the dining room and were dusting the place for fingerprints. Nowadays they didn't have time to investigate burglaries but when a death was involved that was an entirely different matter.

As Doctor Holt went to climb into his car, the police sergeant said, 'Doctor could you tell me a little about Mrs. Eastwood's condition. We don't want to harm her health in any way.'

'Of course. Mrs. Eastwood has a weak heart, but she is receiving treatment and as long as she takes her medication her prognosis is good. She has to take regular, gentle exercise and avoid stress as much as possible. I'd keep the interviews with her short; not more than half an hour at a time, so that she doesn't become exhausted.'

'We'll do that, Doctor.'

'Good, she'll be awake in a couple of hours, but she does need a rest after the night she's had.' The doctor slammed his car door and started the engine.

The sergeant turned back to the investigation. 'Let's just check one more time on the body to see if there's any identification.'

A few hours later Annabel appeared downstairs and Sergeant Rose interviewed her in the kitchen, while P.C. Jones took notes.

'I heard a noise downstairs. My son Marty had gone to Oxford, so I knew it wasn't him. What I should've done was to call the police. I don't know why I didn't. I picked up the torch I keep by my bed.'

'Was it this one?' He held up the long black torch, encased in a plastic evidence bag.

'Yes. It was dark, but when I went into the dining room he came towards me. I couldn't see his face. I mean his features but I struck him with the torch, twice I think and he crumpled to the floor. That's when I ran next door and they called the police for me.'

'How come you didn't see his face?'

'His face was covered. He was wearing a balaclava I think.'

'Ah yes, the intruder had his face covered. Can you tell me if the balaclava could have come from this house?'

Annabel paused, 'Well I did buy my son one a couple of years back. He was doing a lot of work outside.

'Ah I see. Our problem is there's no evidence of a break in.'

'But there must be.'

'Perhaps you left the door open or a window?'

'No, I always lock up very carefully, especially when I'm on my own.'

'Well Mrs. Eastwood, that'll be all for now. We'll prepare your statement. In the meantime have you contacted your son?'

'No not yet, but I will do. He won't be pleased about having to come back, but never mind.'

***

Sam went home and waited and waited but Rob neither phoned or came round.

'Hi Gemma. I don't know what to do,' she said into the phone. 'I still haven't heard from him. Something's wrong.'

'Ok, I'll come over and we'll go to the police station. They won't do anything for a while, but it'll make you feel better.'

True to her word Gemma honked the horn on her car outside Sam's house within ten minutes. It was nearing eleven in the evening and Sam fleetingly thought about the noise disturbing her neighbours, but she was too worried, so she just picked up her bag and rushed out.

At the police station they patiently took her statement and told her not to worry. 'Some men are commitment phobic and if it was getting serious, he may have just legged it.' The constable said.

They were just about to leave and Sam delved into her bag and took out a photograph of Rob. 'I thought this might help.'

***

The next day Annabel Eastwood decided to go to the police station to sign her statement.

'Good morning, Mrs. Eastwood. Let me take you to Sergeant Rose,' said P.C. Jones.

As they walked through the office, Annabel stopped and paused and picked up a photograph from one of the desks. 'Why've you a photograph of my son and who's that girl he's with?'

P.C. Jones examined the photograph and paled. 'I'm not sure why that photograph is there,' he said. 'Let's find Sergeant Rose and we'll see if we can sort it out.'

He showed Annabel into an interview room and left her on her own. It was a good ten minutes later when Sergeant Rose entered the room.

'I'm afraid we've some bad news for you.'

'What bad news can you have? Yesterday someone broke into my house and frightened the life out of me and I've killed him. How will I ever live with that? What bad news can you possibly have?'

Sergeant Rose and P.C. Jones exchanged a quick glance.

'O.K. you'd better tell me then.'

'Well Mrs. Eastwood. We have reason to believe that the intruder was your son.'

'But that's ridiculous. It can't be. What would he be doing, wearing a balaclava, indoors?'

'Yes, that's an interesting question. There is of course one way we can determine whether it was your son. Will you come and look at the body?'

'But why do you think it's him?'

'He looks very similar to the photograph you looked at on the way to this room,' said Sergeant Rose.

Mrs. Eastwood turned pale, 'Yes, of course I'll come'.

'I'll just go and arrange that and P.C. Jones will sit with you.'
***

'Yes, this is Samantha Talbot. Is he alright? Yes I'll come straight down.' Sam put the phone down it seemed they'd found Rob, but he must've been in an accident because the police officer didn't want to talk on the phone.

As soon as she arrived, she was shown into a room, where Sergeant Rose was already seated at the desk and her photo of Rob was on the table in front of him.

'What's happened? Is he alright? I've been worried sick?' Sam said.

'All in good time. There are some routine questions I need to ask about your boyfriend, Rob Vyners. Is that Robert Vyners?' he asked showing the photo, she'd brought in the day before.

Sergeant Rose carried a certain authority that compelled her to answer.

'Yes, that's him,' she said.

'And when did he go missing?'

'Well we were at the Oxford Rest Hotel on Saturday but when I woke up on Sunday, at about seven, he was gone. His overnight things were still in the room.'

'Perhaps you can tell me why you didn't report him missing for another sixteen hours?'

'No, I can't. I just thought he would ring me or come round to my place, but he didn't. I was feeling very sluggish all day.'

'Heavy night, was it?' Sergeant Rose asked without a hint of criticism.

'No, not particularly. I think we shared a bottle of wine between the two of us.'

'So, why do you think you were feeling sluggish?'

'I really don't know. The only time I've ever felt a bit like that was when I had a pre-med for my appendix op.'

Changing tack completely Sergeant Rose asked, 'Why didn't you just call round to his place?'

Sam could feel the colour rising and crawling over her face. She hesitated but knew she'd have to tell the truth.

'I know you're going to think I'm stupid, but I don't know where he lives. He never told me. Of course I asked and asked, so he promised I could spend the night at his, this coming weekend. It couldn't be before then because he's decorating.'

'It's not up to me to judge whether or not you are stupid, Miss Talbot. My job is just to see that you tell the truth. Did you think it strange that he didn't give you his address?'

'Well I suppose I did a bit, but he's very persuasive. Gemma, my friend thought he was married, but I believed him when he said he wasn't.'

'As I've just said, I need to search for the truth and I wondered if you'll let the doctor take a blood test. It would be a great help and if you've nothing to hide there'd be no harm.'

'I hate having blood tests, but I suppose so, although even if I'd been paralytic I think the alcohol would have gone by now.'

Sergeant Rose nodded his acceptance of her agreement and went straight onto another question. 'And how did you meet him?'

'He was working in an Estate Agents and I'm looking to buy a house, since I inherited some money from my Aunt.'

'Hmmm, I see. Now do you know a Martin Eastwood?'

'No, why should I? Please have you found Rob? Is he all right?'

'Miss Talbot, I'm afraid we've found a body, who may or may not be your boyfriend. We would like you to come and look as soon as we've done the blood test.'

***

'Well this is an interesting one Sir. One body and two identities. Who do you think is telling the truth?' said P.C. Jones.

'Now that's a good question. Pop round to see Gemma. Do it now while we're keeping an eye on Talbot. See if she backs up her story and just ask for Rob's address and see what she says. I'm going to interview Mrs. Eastwood again.'

Mrs. Eastwood sobs could be heard from outside the interview room. Her tea was untouched and her eyes were raw.

'Mrs. Eastwood, I'm sorry but I need to ask you a couple of questions. Can you tell me what car Martin drove and the number plate number if you know it?'

'It was a green Renault. AL09 NVQ.'

'That'll be very helpful. Now can I ask if you know a Robin Vyners?'

Mrs. Eastwood stopped sobbing and looked carefully at Sergeant Rose. My son was Robin Martin Vyners before we adopted him. We did everything we could for him but he became an angry young man. Of course I loved him and his early life had been atrocious, but sometimes there was a look in his eyes that made me just a little bit scared.'

'Had you had an argument with him on the night he died.'

Mrs. Eastwood drew herself up straight. 'I don't know what you're trying to imply but NO. He was

101

happy. He was going to a conference and he said this weekend was going to turn his life around.'

'Thank you, Mrs. Eastwood. I'll get one of my officers to drop you home.'

'No thank you. I'd rather walk.' She said standing up and picking up her handbag.

***

The next day Mrs. Eastwood and Sam were back at the police station. 'I'd like to introduce you both. Angela Eastwood, this is Sam Talbot. I think you'll find you have more in common than you think.'

Angela and Sam acknowledged each other and sat back to listen to Sergeant Rose.

'As we now know, Robin Vyners, also known as Martin Eastwood, died last week by the hand of Mrs. Eastwood, who took him to be an intruder. She says that his face was covered. We have no way of proving this, but he was wearing a balaclava when we arrived. We found no identification on his body. Whilst it is possible that Mrs. Eastwood could have hidden this, it was found in his car just round the corner.'

'But why did he come home dressed in black and wearing a balaclava? It doesn't make sense,' asked Mrs. Eastwood.

'You had recently been diagnosed with a weak heart and he is your heir. We believe that he intended to frighten you and leave you to die. What he didn't realize was that having a weak heart isn't synonymous with lacking courage. He just didn't imagine you'd attack him.'

Sam tried to ask a question but her mouth was dry. This was the man she'd been dating and Gemma had said all along she'd thought he was a wrong 'un.

'And was this girl a part of all this – trying to get my money?' asked Mrs. Eastwood.

Sergeant Rose turned towards Sam, 'We think you were his alibi.'

'But I would never...' croaked Sam.

'Don't worry. We don't think you knew anything about it. We think he took you to a hotel, wined and dined you and drugged you. He then slipped out of the hotel to frighten his mother. We think his intention was to be there when you woke up and then you would have sworn he was with you all night.'

Sam put both hands up to her face. 'Oh that's so awful and I trusted him. I can't believe he'd do that.'

'We know that he was after his adoptive mother's money but there's a good possibility he was after yours as well. You did say you'd just inherited from your Aunt. It's better to face this now because otherwise you'll take longer to deal with it.'

'Thank you Sergeant for explaining what happened,' said Mrs. Eastwood. I did love my son you know. If he'd have asked for money I'd have given it.'

'I'm sure you would. You need to think of him as a troubled lad, who never recovered from his early life. As there has been a death I'm afraid this will have to be passed on to the CPS but I very much doubt there will be any prosecutions.'

The two women walked out of the police building without saying a word. What was there to say? Gemma was waiting outside to pick up Sam and leaned over to open the passenger door.

As she was about to get in, Mrs Eastwood spoke to her.

'Just between ourselves, did you know what he was planning? I'll always wonder.'

'No', replied Sam. 'I would never have gone out with him if I'd known.'

'She didn't know,' confirmed Gemma.

'Well for the rest of my life I'll have to live with what I've done, but it may be that your life will be better because of it,' Mrs Eastwood said and she turned and walked away, disappearing into the crowds.

Harmony

Sadie stood in the graveyard huddled in an old coat, her hair hidden under a grey fur hat. She stooped a little to give the impression of age. Her eyes were wet from the piercing wind which stirred the leaves on the ground. She watched her family from a few graves away where Sylvie was enfolded at the centre of the group as always. There was a certain rightness, an order to the world, that they should be in the same place at the same time, after so many months of discord.

Sylvie had always come first. She was the expected baby. Mr. and Mrs. Carter had been awaiting the afterbirth but had received a second baby. Quickly recovering they'd made sure their girls were well fed and educated to the highest level but their eyes only shone for Sylvie. Where Sylvie was bright and sparkly, Sadie was intelligent and deep. Realizing that she could never compete with her favoured sister, she turned her back on the gift of music that both twins had, and chose to study law at London University.

She enjoyed the solving of puzzles, the reading of people and presenting of arguments and soon became respected in her field. Sadie was unaware of the picture of elegance she made in the courtroom. Her sister also achieved well. After Music College she was accepted by the London Philharmonic Orchestra and while Sadie wore Armani suits, Sylvia wore dresses of silk and diamante.

Gradually there became a certain peace within the family and Sadie accepted that Sylvie's accomplishments were always spoken about first, but at least hers were now mentioned. Family get togethers became more pleasurable.

There was also a certain symmetry to their linked lives. Both girls left home within a week of each other and one month later they both visited their parents proudly driving their first cars. Sadie drove up in a functional black Honda Jazz, which shone with cleanliness, while Sylvie drove up in a bright red Mini, splattered with mud. There was a consensus amongst the rest of the family that both were good first cars, although perhaps the Mini was more fun to drive.

'Why did you choose black? It's not very exciting,' challenged Sylvie.

'It's just a car. It gets me from A to B without breaking down.'

'What do you mean it's just a car? I love my Mini.'

'Not enough to keep it clean.'

'Don't be so boring.'

In the following years both girls brought back various young men. Sadie's were sensible and Sylvie's were often creative people with non-conformist hair styles. And then Sadie fell in love. Oliver was extremely bright, with so many interests, although some thought he was a little brutal in the way he prosecuted the accused; others felt it was a requirement of the job.

Oliver won the court case where she was acting on the defendant's team, but she was still delighted when he asked her out. Soon they were inseparable.

'Come to the Lake District,' he said and so they missed the monthly family get together.

They spent every weekend together and the following month they were in London enjoying a play. Oliver whipped Sadie away to Barcelona the next month and so it was four months later that Sadie took Oliver home to meet the family.

'So who is this darling man?' Sylvie asked, as they walked in the door.

Sadie felt so proud to be bringing home her special man. 'This is Oliver and this is my twin sister, Sylvie.' Never had she felt such completeness and happiness. Oliver greeted Sylvie politely. Mr. and Mrs. Carter were delighted that Sadie was so happy.

'So Oliver would you like to come to the Barbican and hear me play next weekend?' Sylvie asked.

'We're going to Bath for the weekend Sylvie,' Sadie answered.

Sylvie tilted her head to one side and leaned towards Oliver, 'Oh do Oliver. It would be so lovely to have you there.'

'Sylvie, leave it,' Mrs. Carter said. 'They're busy.'

Later Sadie said to Oliver, 'Sylvie seems to have taken to you. She was very pushy that we go to see her perform next week.'

'Was she? I thought she was charming.'

It was not long before Oliver was in agreement with the rest of the family, drawn to worship Sylvie. He started to listen to her music, and one day Sadie picked up his phone and found that Sylvie and Oliver were texting.

'What's going on?' she asked him. 'Why are you in contact with Sylvie?'

'I'm so sorry. I'm really fond of you, but I love her. She's so different, so exciting. When she plays a melody on her violin she lifts my soul. I could spend my life listening to her.'

Sadie went home to lick her wounds and Mr. and Mrs. Carter did their best to comfort her right up to the point that Sylvie and Oliver turned up.

'You're going to have to accept the situation. Sylvie is always welcome here too. They're in love,' Mr. Carter said.

As they came in through the front door Sadie slipped out of the back. She passed Oliver's BMW. He had two cars; the BMW was for longer journeys and the orange MG was for short fun drives, although he never drove in the centre of London. Sadie went back to her flat and after a sleepless night she made some difficult decisions. 'I'm going to move on. If my family is going to welcome Sylvie in spite of her betraying me then I will cut myself away from them.' She promptly put her flat on the market and moved to Manchester.

With a new flat and job Sadie was very busy, but soon she settled into her new life. While sorting out her flat she found her old flute and decided to see if she could still play. Her music was not of her sister's standard. She dug out a simple piece of music and dressed in comfortable pyjamas, with her golden hair tumbling down her back she picked up her flute.

The music flowed from her as if she'd never stopped playing. Sadie felt something positive had come from her break with the family. She had her music back.

Suddenly there was a loud knock on her door. 'Who could that be?' she thought.

There in front of her was a young man in jeans and a faded T shirt.

'I'm Dave from the flat upstairs.'

'Oh I'm sorry, was I too loud?'

108

'Not at all,' he replied. 'I play with a couple of others in a small group and I heard your wonderful playing. If you're free tomorrow come along to The Feathers and see us. Bring your flute.' He smiled as he left to go back upstairs.

'How ridiculous,' she thought, but the next day after work she took her flute and went to find The Feathers.

It was early and the pub wasn't crowded. Dave spotted her immediately and introduced her to Gerry who played double bass and Marlene who played the drums. Dave who sang and played the guitar persuaded her to join in and they played a Beatles' number, Eleanor Rigby, in perfect harmony. In a million years Sadie would never have thought she would enjoy playing music in a pub, with strangers, as much as she did.

Soon she was working hard all week and spending Friday and Saturday nights with her new friends. Dave was a kind sensitive man and she enjoyed his company.

One day as she came out of the courts to grab a quick lunch she found her father waiting for her.

'This behaviour has got to stop,' he greeted her.

'What exactly do you mean by that?'

'Come home. Make it up with your sister. She and your mother are very upset by your behaviour.'

'Father, I'm not coming home. There's no room for me in your lives. She betrayed me in the worst way possible and you both took her side. I can't live in her shadow anymore.'

'You're not in her shadow. If it's any consolation I think she's not as keen on Oliver as she was.'

'I don't care. I'm happy here without her or him. I'm sorry. I'll come back when I'm ready. You all hurt me and when I needed your support you weren't there for me. Please go back home and leave me alone.'

'You can't stop being part of the family. She's your sister. We're your parents.'

'Sisters don't take each other's boyfriends. Parents shouldn't condone such behaviour. I've moved a long way away to find some peace and I've found it. Go home and enjoy your favoured daughter.' Sadie turned and walked back into the courtrooms. She'd have to ask her junior to go and get a sandwich for her.

Although shaken by her father's visit she stuck to her resolve. She wasn't going to allow any of them to hurt her again.

It was a week later that she switched on the television to find her sister being interviewed by a late night chat show host. Sylvie looked wonderful. She was wearing a slinky black dress and was going to play out the show.

'Is there someone special in your life at the moment Sylvie?' the interviewer asked.

'Oh no, I have to work so hard and travel such a lot, so there's not really much time for any of that.' Sylvie purred.

'I wonder what Oliver will make of that,' thought Sadie. She stayed up and listened to her sister lead the playing of Pachabelle's Canon. It was beautiful.

Sadie continued working hard and playing in the little band. There was a regular crowd at the Feathers and some of her work colleagues started coming on a Friday night.

In between songs she heard her phone ring and found a quiet place to take the call. It was from Oliver.

'She's dumped me,' he said. 'Can you believe that she broke us up and then dumped me?'

'I'm sorry Oliver. It hurts like hell now, but you'll get over it. Trust me. I know.'

'Look, would you like to meet up?'

'Sorry. I'm really sorry, but I'm completely off men and there's no way back for us. I wish you well Oliver. Goodbye.'

'Are you really off men?' Dave said. 'Sorry I didn't mean to eavesdrop.'

Sadie held up her phone. 'Ex boyfriend. Went off with my twin and now she's dumped him. He's not happy but I'm not getting involved.'

'We're not all the same. Come out with me for a meal tomorrow.'

With a great deal of trepidation Sadie accepted and soon realized that he could become more than just a friend.

The following week when she came home from work on the Monday the phone was ringing.

'There's been a terrible accident,' her father said. 'Your sister has been killed by a hit and run driver. You'll have to come home.'

'Oh how awful, but I don't think I can come.'

That evening she went and discussed it with Dave, who thought she'd regret not going back. He offered to come with her but she said no, she'd go by herself. And she'd go, she thought, but secretly. She had no intention of staying with her parents.

When Dave had gone she switched the television on and caught the news. Her sister's death was reported briefly, because she'd been a minor celebrity. The police were appealing for the driver of the orange sports car to come forward.

Immediately she thought of Oliver's car, but it couldn't be.

Sadie slipped a note through Dave's door and hired a car to drive to London. She didn't want to be recognised. When she arrived she booked into an anonymous hotel, in a nearby town, under a false name.

The next day Sadie sat in a cafe opposite the Old Bailey courts, where she knew Oliver was due to appear. When she saw him enter the building she made her way to his flat, knowing he would be tied up for several hours. She put on an old coat, gloves and grey fur hat that she'd bought from a charity shop. The outfit completely changed her appearance. Then she made her way to his garage, and took out the key from behind a loose brick, where it was always kept. In just a few minutes she established that the orange MG was not there. The shiny navy BMW was alone.

With no idea where it could be, she found a public phone box and phoned the police. Pretending to be Oliver's wife she reported it stolen. They took the number and then told her that her husband had already reported it. 'Of course,' she thought he would have reported it.

'I'd suggest you look at the bumper when you find it,' she said quickly and then hung up.'

She knew Oliver was a very clever, ruthless man, who'd been publicly humiliated by her sister. She went back to the hotel and there she stayed until the day of the funeral.

It was bitterly cold in the churchyard. Sadie was dressed in the grey hat and old coat. She blended into the background. The vicar was saying prayers as the final ceremony unfolded. Individual disjointed words floated over to where she stood. She said her own prayers. When they'd all said their goodbyes the family passed by not noticing Sadie. At the edge of the churchyard there was a commotion. Plain clothes policemen were taking Oliver away. They'd found his car parked on one of the most notorious estates in London with the keys in the ignition. Although Oliver had reported the car missing there had been no fingerprints on the driving wheel or doors. There was a big dent in the front of the car on the right hand side. He'd obviously hoped that joy riders would take it away and burn it out. Perhaps they might have done but for the England - France football match and the call from his non-existent wife, which had focused the police to search more vigorously.

Sadie stayed in the churchyard for a while. She went and stood by her sister's grave and then the tears began to fall. She sobbed for all the years her sister wouldn't have and for the friendship they could now never mend. She sobbed until she realized that she was shivering with cold and the light had slipped quietly away. Briefly the music that her sister last played filled her mind. Nobody deserved to be murdered just because they'd behaved badly but there was nothing she could do. She'd helped to get her sister justice. Tonight she would go back to her family and try to restore a fragile harmony, but in a few days she'd return to Manchester and be where she wanted to be, with Dave.

One More Chance

'No mother, I'm not giving up my room. Why don't you?' Terri shouted.

'Don't be ridiculous, she always stays in your room,' replied Susan trying to keep her voice calm.

'Well it's time that stopped.'

'How can you be so unkind to your Gran?'

'Excuse me! But how can you be so unkind? She's your responsibility. Not mine. What's the difference of you moving out of your room and me moving out of mine? Anyway every time she comes she goes through my things.'

'Don't be silly. She's not like that.' Susan hesitated, *surely not*, she thought.

'I think I'd know. She goes through all my clothes. Anyway I'm not moving out. I need my space, especially when you two start watching all that mush on TV.'

'And I'm not having you dictate to me what will happen in my house.'

'It's not just your house. It's dad's too! You've driven him away and if you don't stop being such a bitch I'll go. I'd rather live with him anyway!' Terri slammed out of the room.

Susan held her head in her hands and a curtain of blonde hair swung forward. She knew she'd not handled that well and on reflection she could see

Terri's point of view. She didn't want to give up her space either and she didn't feel like Christmas. Susan, sat there nursing her coffee, but the warmth of the mug brought little comfort.

'Of course,' Terri said sticking her head round the door, 'We could turn the dining room into a room for Gran. Now there will only be three of us for Christmas lunch we can eat in here. I'll move the table and chairs to the side of the room and you can get the chair bed from the front room.'

Susan was about to object when she realized this was actually a very plausible idea. They set to work and soon the chair bed was set up and made and one of the dining room chairs was being used as a bedside table. The rest of the room was rearranged so that the furniture was all on the other side allowing plenty of room to walk around. Terri rearranged the contents of the dresser so that there was space for her Gran to put her clothes and then they decorated the room with bright Christmas decorations.

Christmas Eve came and Gran arrived.

'You're in here Gran,' Terri said pushing open the door to the brightly decorated room.

'Oh thank you for being so thoughtful. My arthritis does make your stairs so painful. This is just perfect. It's so good you have a downstairs bathroom.'

Susan breathed a sigh of relief. She'd thought about not inviting Gran for Christmas, but then she'd have been on her own and it wasn't Gran's fault that she and Barry had split up. They had a quiet evening catching up on each other's news.

Christmas morning dawned, cold but bright. Everyone tried to be cheerful but the house was quiet without Barry and they were all feeling the gap. They unwrapped their presents and Susan disappeared to the kitchen to get on with the meal. It was ridiculous that she was doing a full Christmas meal for just the three of them, but she didn't want to admit that her world had changed.

Eating in the kitchen was cosy. Terri had decorated the table with crackers and napkins and Susan produced masses of food. They toasted each other with a small glass of wine and then settled to a companionable quiet as they ate their meal.

Suddenly there was a knock on the door and then it opened. Barry stood there with a few beautifully wrapped presents. Susan was about to ask him what he thought he was playing at when Terri leapt up and gave him a bear hug.

'Oh Daddy, I've missed you.' Susan hadn't heard Terri use the word daddy for years. These days it was usually dad. His deep brown, puppy dog eyes, framed with those thick lashes, looked at her plaintively.

'Oh OK. Go and get your father a plate Terri. You'd best go and get yourself a chair Barry,' and as he left the room she slipped the wine bottle in the fridge and placed a fresh glass and some lemonade near the vacant space. Gran looked at the bottle without commenting and helped herself to a few more sprouts.

'Happy Christmas son,' she said when he carried the chair into the room and bent and kissed her.

Terri came to life and told her dad all about their Christmas preparations and her idea for Gran to have the dining room.

'Yes it's been lovely. The only thing I miss, is when I stayed in your room, Terri, I used to tidy up your clothes like I did when you were a toddler. Do you remember being sent up to tidy your room and we used to do it together? But I guess you're too grown up for that now anyway.'

Susan could see the look on Terri's face of, 'So that's what Gran had been doing.' She gave her daughter a secret smile.

'Course I remember Gran. You've always been great. I'm so glad we're all here together.'

The meal was surprisingly pleasant. At one point Barry went to the fridge and brought back the bottle of wine. Susan was about to explode when she felt Gran's tissue paper hand give hers a squeeze. Barry topped up his mother's glass and then Susan's.

'What about me?' asked Terri.

'I thought we might share the lemonade,' he said putting the bottle back in the fridge.

'Oh OK.'

'Well that was a lovely meal. Thank you so much for letting me stay. It's pretty bleak in my bedsit.'

'You shouldn't be in a bedsit. You should be here. If she hadn't kicked you out we'd all be happy again,' and Terri sent her mother a look of almost hatred.

There was silence.

'You need to tell her Barry. She's old enough,' said Gran.

Barry went white and took a deep breath. 'Your mum's been an absolute saint.' He took another breath and then looked at Terri straight in the eye. 'I'm an alcoholic. I've messed up so many times, lost jobs, failed to go to your school performances, spent money we couldn't afford and kept dragging us down.'

'You're not. You're not. You're not violent or aggressive. You're nothing like Phil Mitchell in Eastenders.'

Barry smiled, 'Not all alcoholics are violent. Some are. Some, like me, just cause mayhem, disrupt all the careful plans couples have. We were going to have two children, but your mum had to go out to work and pay off my debts. She gave me one last chance about ten times.'

'You should've told me,' Terri said turning towards Susan.

'How could I? He was your hero. Always. But you are my baby and I wanted to protect you.' A tear slipped down her cheek.

Suddenly Terri was giving her a bear hug.

'So many things make sense now. I should've seen,' Terri said.

'No, neither of us wanted you to see.' Barry replied. 'I want you all to know that I've not had any alcohol for 3 months and eight days. That's one day after your mother finally came to her senses and said enough is enough. I know I've blown it with your mum, but I still want to be a good dad to you and I know the only way I can do that is by not drinking.'

'That's a good achievement, son,' said Gran. 'I'm very proud of you. Now I think we should go into the front room and open the presents your dad's brought us.'

Barry passed round his presents and Gran and Terri gave him theirs. Susan went quietly to the cupboard behind the television and took out a wrapped parcel.

'It's nothing much, so don't get excited,' she said as she handed Barry his present.

'I didn't expect anything. Thank you.' It was a book by his favourite author.

Later Barry insisted on doing the washing up and disappeared to the kitchen. After he'd been gone just a few minutes Susan started to worry about the wine in the fridge. She made the excuse of going to make some tea and left Gran and Terri watching some dreadful old film. Terri grimaced at her as she left the room but Susan just smiled.

In the kitchen Barry was immersed in a pile of plates and washing up liquid.

'I've just come to make some tea.'

'You've come to check up on me and I don't blame you. Let's not start lying to each other now. If I thought there was any chance for us, I'd suggest that if I could stay off drink for a year, you let me come home. But there isn't any chance is there?'

'I cannot live with a drunk.'

'I know that. I couldn't believe it when you kicked me out. I always thought you'd be there to sort out all my mess. It was the best thing you could ever

119

have done for me. And then it hit me. I'd chucked away everything; everyone I love.'

Susan knew that this was one of her life's crossroads. If she took him back he might start drinking again, but she still loved him and Terri was not the only one who pined for him.

All life is a gamble, she thought and then she took the step that would change their lives for better or worse. 'You can come home now, but if one drop of alcohol touches your lips you'll be back out so quickly you won't know what's hit you. Do you understand?'

'I understand,' he said solemnly.

'I've missed you so much,' Susan said holding out her arms.

Barry leapt over to her and she let out a scream of delight as he lifted her into the air and twirled her round. Gran and Terri rushed to the kitchen to see what the noise was and saw the joy on their two faces.

'Come on Gran,' Terri said linking her arm. 'Time for us to open the chocolates and finish watching that mushy film.'

'Or we could watch one of your DVDs. I'd like to keep up to date with what my lovely granddaughter enjoys.'

The Mist

The mist had stayed all day, hiding the village from the rest of the world. Usually the sun broke through late morning and the white veil disappeared into blue skies, but today there was a dampness that hung in the air which mirrored the darkness in Celia's heart.

It was exactly a year ago today that Celia had almost grasped her dream. Something she'd longed for and prayed for, but it was snatched away literally minutes before it became a reality.

So today was just a day that she had to get through, like so many days before; and if it was a white day where all the colours paled into blandness, that suited her just fine. Occasionally cars crawled past her house with their lights blaring out ineffectively but the world was quiet with all the usual noises seemingly flattened.

Celia's husband returned from work at six in the evening.

'It's really strange,' he said, 'that we've been covered with this mist all day. Just outside the village it's clear. There's not a trace of it. Don't you think it unusual?'

'Yes, I suppose it is. Still it must clear soon,' replied Celia.

Her mind lapsed back to a year ago. Her husband had been in America, working on a long term project. Spending months on her own had been part of their marriage. She didn't mind it so much now, but when she was younger she'd found the loneliness almost unbearable. The phone call she'd received out of the blue last year had sent her into a fluster. After the years of hoping to see her secret son, he was going to visit her. She'd tidied the house from top to bottom and put on her prettiest frock. Of course she'd never told her husband about him. How could she? All those years ago when she'd been so isolated in a little village, hardly knowing anyone and Jack had been across the Atlantic, had made her vulnerable. Someone had offered her warmth and she'd taken it. Waiting for her visitor she'd paced up and down the house, her heart buzzing with excitement and anticipation.

She'd kept looking at her watch. He'd have to come through Chester and then along the A51, turning right towards her village. Then he'd pass Mr. Crimble's place and pull up in her drive. Mr. Crimble was her nearest neighbour, although he was a five minute walk away and on the other side of the road. His place had been a little run down and then he'd won the lottery and started spending his money by smartening up his property. He'd pulled up the white wooden fence and had a high brick wall built at the front of his property, with big iron gates that were operated by an electronic control.

Celia had thought the change unnecessary because living in the country they were rarely troubled with the crime problems that city people had, but she understood Mr. Crimble's lifelong desire to have a walled garden.

Her visitor was late but Celia didn't worry until the sound of the siren pierced the silence and the blue lights could be seen flashing down the road. Then an awful feeling of dread overwhelmed her. Logically she told herself this could have nothing to do with her, but after half an hour she went and fetched her coat. She stepped out into the night and the coldness clawed at her face as she made her way towards the parked police car. It was outside Mr. Crimble's house. Soon she could see his smart new wall had been demolished on one side and pressed up against the remains was a small Citroen, with its bonnet crushed to half its normal size. Through the window of the car, on the passenger side, she could see a bunch of yellow roses lying on the floor, which were remarkably untouched.

The policeman at the site was not amused with her interest. 'Excuse me madam, could you step back. This is a scene of an accident and there will be an investigation.'

'I'm sorry officer. I was expecting a visitor; a Mr. Thomas Bailey. He's not arrived and I just had an awful feeling. I don't suppose you know the name of the person in the car.'

Celia had been sent back to her house and soon a police woman had knocked on the door to give her the bad news. It had been Thomas in the car and she would never see him.

The pain had not eased in the past year. She'd put on a brave face because Jack didn't know about Thomas and there was no point in causing him pain now. All those years ago she'd done what she'd thought was right and given away her baby, even though every part of her had cried out against it.

Celia had slipped into the back of the church when Thomas was being buried and sat quietly through the service. She could not have the luxury of sobbing like Thomas's mother, nor the privilege of paying Thomas a tribute as his father had done. She learned how popular he was and that he had a dog called Zorro. She learned his favourite colour had been yellow and that he'd just been accepted for a new job teaching science at a University.

If only he hadn't come to visit her. If only he hadn't come on that day. If only the other car hadn't been on the wrong side of the road making him swerve into Mr. Crimble's wall. If only Mr. Crimble hadn't built a wall.

Now she looked up at Jack sitting comfortably in his favourite chair, innocent of all her anguish and knew she had to get out of the house.

'I'm just going for a walk,' she said grabbing her coat and making a quick exit before he could offer to come with her.

The mist surrounded her immediately as she walked along the road. It was so thick it was difficult to see where she was and she felt quite disorientated. Just as she came to Mr. Crimble's house the outline of a man emerged.

'I knew you'd come today. I just wanted to see you once,' he said. 'I know you're still grieving for what might have been; the time we could've spent together, but you mustn't.'

'Thomas,' she said breathlessly, hardly daring to speak.

'It's strange, but I knew you would know me. In the world where I am now truth is transparent. I know about your life and why you gave me up. I understand and I know how much you've thought of me and regretted not telling Jack about me.'

'There are so many questions I want to ask you. I want to know all about you.'

'I'm so sorry but there's no time. Just know that I'm all right now and I had a happy life. You must live your tomorrow, not regret what you can't change.' As he spoke his figure drifted back into the darkness and although she called his name there was no reply.

When she re-entered the house Jack was snoozing in his chair and she gently woke him so they could go to bed. Surprisingly Celia slept soundly. She dreamt of a little boy, with dark curly hair, like her own, starting school, playing football with his friends climbing trees and cycling downhill with his legs sticking out and the pedals whirring round uncontrollably. A kaleidoscope of images came to her.

In the morning she decided she would tell Jack the whole story. It was time.

'When I went out for a walk last night a strange thing happened,' she started.

'Don't be daft Celia. There was a thick fog. You didn't go out last night,' he said picking up the Times, shaking it out and starting to read, effectively blocking her out.

Celia picked up her coffee and went out into the garden. There was no mist now. It was a beautiful day and the sun was shining brightly. She walked to the bottom of the garden thinking of Thomas and all the wonderful images she'd seen in her dreams. Could they possibly be him or was her mind just playing tricks? How would she ever know?

Exactly a year later she was in her garden again when she noticed at the far corner of her vegetable plot a small bush was growing that she'd not seen before. A single yellow rose flowered on the bush but there were several tight buds which promised more to come.

She touched the flower's silky petals. It felt as though Thomas had sent her a message. She decided that she would actively embrace her future and one day she would be with her son again.

'Thank you, Thomas,' she said as the sun emerged from behind a cloud.

Wanted

She ran down the street with her hair flying behind her. The pavements were shiny and the street lights reflected in the grey slabs.

Marcia turned the corner and pressed herself against the wall to listen for footsteps. There were none. She looked around her, there was nowhere to hide. Just at that moment a bus came round the corner. Marcia took the decision to jump on it. She paid her fare and sat down, relieved to be away from danger. Soon the bus stopped. She stepped down. She didn't see the small thickset man who jumped off the bus into the darkness, silently behind her.

Marcia walked along the unlit road unhurriedly. There were no sinister footsteps now. Her tiny tee shirt showed her midriff between the short skirt and a wide leather belt. Her hair draped like a curtain across her face, but she could see her way in the night by the light of a bright moon, peeping through a gap in the gathering clouds.

Suddenly she heard a squelching sound. The realization that there was a grass verge and the smell of stale tobacco hit her at the same moment. She was about to turn round when a large hand went over her mouth, making it difficult to breathe. Marcia could feel her heart pounding so loudly that it echoed in her ears.

'Bitch,' he whispered in her ear. 'You bitch. I'll teach you. You think you're so clever.'

She tried to scream but the man's chubby fingers were pressing fiercely against her lips.

Suddenly she wished she'd been wearing something more substantial.

'Why had she been so complacent?'

The long knife slipped smoothly out of its soft leather sheath without any sound. The thrust upwards pierced resistant skin and she felt the warm sticky substance she knew to be blood, against her skin.

The body curled onto the ground into a foetus position. It shook gently for several seconds and then lay still on the hard pavement. At that moment another shower started. Heavy rain splashed down, diluting the blood and washing it away into the gutter.

The knife was quickly cleaned on the deceased's tee shirt and slipped away to its hidden place. Footsteps ran from the scene. Under the cover of the night only the moon saw the murderer disappear into the small grey terraced house at 72 Tudor Close. Clothes went straight into the open fireplace and firelighters were poked beneath to make them burn quickly. Then beneath the power jet shower the last remnants of death were washed away.

'Get the scene covered quickly before all the forensics are washed away,' barked D.I. Thorne.

It was late and he'd been looking forward to a quiet night in. Still he thought he was luckier than the corpse lying on the pavement. Looked like a stabbing but you could never tell until the lab had done their bit.

The road was now teaming with people. Tape had been strung across it. Parked cars with blue flashing lights littered the street and white costumed people were taking measurements and photographs, tagging where evidence was found. It was going to be a long night.

Dressed in clean clothes, having cleared the grate and soaked the knife in bleach, everything could return to normal. Then the doorbell screeched.

'Who could that be at this time of night? The body surely couldn't have been found yet.'

'Good evening. I'm Sergeant Jones and this is P.C. Taylor. We're just asking a few questions of everyone on the neighbourhood. May we come in?'

'No, it's very late.'

Jones and Taylor stood at the doorway and having checked the name of the house occupant, continued with their enquiries.

'Have you been in all evening?'

'Yes.'

'Have you seen or heard anything unusual?' asked P.C. Taylor.

'No I haven't and I'm off to bed now, if there's nothing else.'

'No nothing for the moment but we may have to contact you again. Thank you for your time.'

The door closed and Jones and Taylor moved on to the next house.

After they'd gone, the murderer decided it was time to examine the recently acquired phone; an iPhone. 'It's been worth all that trauma to get my hands on it. Why should these rich sods always have the best things? It's beautiful; a white one. To hold one after wanting it for so long feels great and I'd never have been able to buy one.'

Meanwhile Jones and Taylor had been sent back to the station and were examining CCTV footage of the road. It was a tedious job, so they brought a plateful of sandwiches and mugs of tea.

After about half an hour Jones shouted, 'Hold on a minute. I know that face. Number 72 Tudor Drive. Rude idiot who was just off to bed. Do you remember?'

The following day the doorbell rang loudly again.

'We have a warrant to search these premises,' said D.I. Thorne.

'You'd best come in then, hadn't you?'

It took the police less than an hour to find the shiny knife in its leather sheath.

'It's not a crime to own a knife. I never take it out anywhere.'

'Well we'll take it and have it examined,' said D.I. Thorne.

'Fine, you won't find anything on it.'

'You've cleaned it.'

'I didn't say that.'

'But did you remember to clean the inside of the sheath? Nowadays forensics can pick up the smallest traces of blood.' said D.I. Thorne.

Marcia's hair swung forward across her face, but not before the look of realization and fear flashed into her eyes.

Baby Love

'Not long now,' I thought, stroking my oversized stomach. I smiled across at Tim and his hazel eyes crinkled up in response. The Nursery was freshly painted and everything was ready. It could be anytime now. Who can ever tell about these things? My new mother-in-law, Millie, had acted stoically at the news of an early baby. She'd said all the right things, but somehow her enthusiasm was a little dim. Tim on the other hand was so excited.

'Let's get the best car seat buggy,' he said.

'Shouldn't we wait 'til the baby's born,' I suggested.

'Oh no, then I'll be left to buy it on my own, so we can bring her home from hospital. Let's go and get it now.'

He built shelves in the nursery for books and toys and fitted sun screens to both our cars. Then on 15 July the pains started.

'You're only seven months. That's rather early,' Millie said. 'Are you sure you've got your dates right?'

'Absolutely' I gasped picking up my overnight bag. 'C'mon Tim, I'd rather be at the hospital.'

'Ready when you are,' he said. 'Let's go.'

Lottie was born within three hours, weighing in at a healthy 6lbs 2oz and my heart melted with love for her. I made a promise there and then that she would have the best possible life I could give her.

'She's so beautiful,' Tim said, 'just like her mother.' But I was surprised by the fleeting look of sadness that showed in his eyes.

'Yes, very nice,' said Millie. 'Tim, could you pop along and get us a cup of tea? We've been here ages and I'm so thirsty.'

As Tim left to do his mother's bidding, Millie moved closer to the hospital bed and lowered her voice.

'I know that child's not my son's. Shall I tell you how I know?'

'No,' I replied, not wishing the day to be spoiled.

'He had cancer as a child. We were told that the treatment would make him infertile. That's how I know, so whoever you think you are kidding, I know that' she glared at my baby, 'is not my grandchild.'

I took a deep breath, 'Well maybe she's a miracle.'

Tim's face fell as he entered the room. The atmosphere was as sharp as a knife.

'Mother, I'm taking you home. I think you have been stirring things.'

Quickly I made a decision. It was time to fight for my baby's future. Perhaps no other conversation would ever be so important.

'No,' I said, 'there's something I need to tell you.'

'No,' said Tim, 'you really don't have to.'

'Yes I do. Sit down both of you.' I picked up Lottie and gently stroked her face.

'Tim found me crying, one night, outside the cinema. Charles, my boyfriend, if I can call him that, had just dumped me.'

'We don't need to do this,' said Tim.

'Please,' I said. 'I was very upset. I thought Charles was everything I needed - good looking, intelligent, exciting, but he never actually wanted me.

He was seeing a married woman and he wanted someone to cover up the situation. Anyway we never made love and then the night I met Tim, don't ask me how, but we ended up in bed together.'

'Oh yes. Right!' Millie said scathingly.

'I have nothing to hide and I'm really happy for you to have DNA tests done.'

'We don't need any tests done. I love you to pieces and I don't care if she's biologically mine or not,' said Tim.

'And I love you too and if you don't know that yet, you will do soon - because I love you so much.'

Millie's eyes softened. 'Perhaps I've been a little quick to judge. I just didn't want *my* child to be hurt.'

I looked at Tim and the sadness had gone. Then I smiled into Lottie's eyes. It looked like she was going to get the father she deserved.

A New Beginning

Dawn looked at the almost bare pen and the animal cowering in the corner, behind his bedding. His black fur was visibly shivering and large anxious eyes looked directly at her.

'You don't want to be looking at that one,' said Gemma. 'He's had a dreadful time and will need a lot of attention. He'd probably do well with an older person. What you need is the lovely bouncy puppy next door. He'll cheer you up and keep you active.'

Dawn ignored her friend and crouched down. 'Come here boy. Come and say hello.' She kept her voice low and calm and held his direct gaze. There was something dignified about the way he watched her. She felt he was saying, 'I may be frightened but I won't give in'.

The dog took a few steps and halted.

'His name's Jet,' Gemma whispered. 'It's a boring name for an all black dog but we thought we'd stick with it in case it made him feel more comfortable.'

Dawn smiled at her friend and then said, 'Jet, come here boy. Come and say hello, Jet.'

The dog came to the edge of the pen and Dawn poked a finger through the wire and gave his head a stroke. Gemma gave a sigh and took out her keys to unlock the pen.

'Ok, go and say hello to him. That's the best reaction we've had since he came here.'

Within a couple of minutes he was wagging his tail and nestling up to Dawn. There was no doubt it was love at first sight and so Gemma agreed to sign him out to her friend as long as he came back for his final check up on Tuesday.

'Your place will suit him fine. It's quiet. You have a good sized garden and you've got Richmond Park nearby to take him for walks.

That evening Jet was sitting on the sofa with Dawn. She stroked his fur and sighed at the thin patch, which was slowly growing back. 'How could anyone leave a dog so infested with fleas that the dog develops a reaction and licks his skin raw?' she thought. The RSPCA had done a wonderful job rescuing him from neglect and hunger and built him back to a reasonable body weight.

Suddenly the doorbell rang. Jet fled off the sofa and hid behind it. 'It's all right Jet,' Dawn said calmly as she went to answer the door.

'I see you've changed the locks. Oh my goodness, what have you done to the hallway?'

What had once been quite a grand hallway now contained a door blocking off the stairs and a wall with a door that led to the ground floor.

'Good evening, Gerald. I changed the locks when you signed the negative equity over to me to deal with. What I've done with the hallway is therefore none of your business.'

'There's no need to be like that. I've just come round to see you're all right.'

'I've packed the rest of your belongings in these three bin liners. They've been here for what seems like ages. Now if you'll excuse me I'm busy.' Dawn moved the bags out of the hallway and over the threshold.

'Surely we can still talk to each other?'

'You dumped me after five years of living with me; after we'd bought our dream home and just when

135

we were about to start a family. You deserted me for a child, who'd just turned eighteen. You left me to sort out all the debts and just walked away to get on with your new life. No I don't think there's any more to be said. Don't come here again.'

'Maybe I made a mistake,' Gerald said more hesitantly. He ran his hand through the front of his hair. 'I was bowled over by a pretty girl, but she's not you. Can I come in? Could we just have a chat?'

Dawn paused. The she took a deep breath. How she'd missed him. How many days had she cried and refused to even get out of bed. She remembered looking in the mirror and just thinking how old and ugly she was. None of which was true. She remembered thinking she would give just about anything to have him back, but debt problems had forced her to stop wallowing in the past. She'd had to find solutions, and quickly, before the mortgage company foreclosed and the house was taken from her. Luckily, her newly married cousin was looking for a place to live near London and it had seemed an ideal solution for them all.

She looked at his pleading face and her tone softened. 'I think you did make a mistake. We had it all, but it's gone now. I've moved on. Sorry.'

Just at that moment Tom, her cousin's husband, came up to the front door. 'Oh excuse me,' he said as he went past them both.

Gerald looked at the young man in amazement. He was a good ten years younger than Gerald and strikingly good looking. Dawn was about to explain that Anne and Tom had moved in to the top half of the house; that she'd made the house into two flats to help pay the mortgage, but something held her back. Perhaps if he hadn't looked so surprised that he thought she'd found someone new, she might've explained the situation.

'Good-bye Gerald,' she said quietly and closed the door. It wouldn't do him any harm to have his self-esteem blown sideways for once.

Then she went back to Jet and comforted him. 'We've both got a new start and we're going to be happy.' She smiled and gave him a stroke. 'C'mon boy let's go and explore the garden and maybe think of a new name for you.'

Jet followed Dawn out through the French doors and his tail started to wag.

A Christmas Surprise

Jodie fingered the fifty pence in her pocket, which was the absolute last bit of money she possessed. She was going to spend it ringing her Aunt. She would try to get an invite for Christmas, which would give her enough time to find another job. Her Aunt was a busy septuagenarian, but Jodie had a lot of time for her, having spent her university years living under her roof.

She kissed the coin to bring her luck, as she dialled the number.

'Well you can come and house sit for me. I'd really appreciate that, but I'm off to stay with my friend Betty for the holidays. I thought you'd be partying with your friends. Come as soon as you like.' Aunt Doris said.

'Thanks Aunt. Is there something I could be doing to help you, to make myself useful?'

'Oh, I'll make a list,' Doris laughed.

A few days later Jodie was busy painting the dining room in a magnolia colour and listening to a story being told on Radio 4. The last few weeks had been so stressful and she was happy to be in the warm and busy. Aunt Doris was cooking wonderful home cooked meals and Jodie had her small bedroom back from her student days. Remarkably she'd found some of her university work, a few large jumpers and other bits and pieces which made her feel at home.

Losing her job had been awful. Her boss had phoned her at her desk and told her that she would be leaving by the end of the week, with a month's pay in lieu of notice. The world's financial crisis had hit her world and several of her friends had also been made redundant. Shattered she went home to the small flat she shared with Greg.

Expecting tea and sympathy she was completely surprised when he'd said, 'Sorry Jodie, but I already pay more than my share of the bills and I'm not having you sponge off me. You'd better find somewhere else to live because you won't be able to afford this on your own.'

'I have a month's wages coming and I'm sure to find another job in that time,' she replied. 'Besides I pay half the rent and half the bills. In what way don't I pay my share?'

'Well for one thing, when it's my turn to cook I take you out somewhere decent and when it's your turn you serve up shepherd's pie.'

'Why on earth didn't you say something, if I was annoying you?'

'Look Jodie, it's not working. Don't make this any harder than it is. Pack your things and go and stay at a friend's.'

Jodie was proud. She'd stood her ground and slept on the sofa that night. She wasn't landing on a friend without warning. She packed her belongings and phoned Anna to ask if she could stay for a few days.

'Of course you can, Jodie, but it'll have to be just a few days because Alan's parents are coming to stay on Wednesday.'

Later when she was at Anna's it occurred to her that the flat was rented in her name. Tears rolled down her face as she told Anna of Greg's comments. She wanted to hit him and feel his arms around her again, both at the same time. Anna expressed exactly what she was feeling.

'Well if I were you I'd shop him to the landlord. What a jerk!'

Being vindictive was not really part of Jodie's nature, but he'd kicked her out, when she was already upset about losing her job as a graphic designer, so she took a deep breath and phoned the landlord.

'I'm really sorry, love but you do realize you'll lose your deposit as you're not giving me notice. Unless of course you think this Greg Richards would make a good tenant. Would you give him a good reference?'

'Well, he earns enough to pay the rent, but I can't honestly say he's reliable. He's very careless with other people's property and he doesn't know how to wash up or put a vacuum cleaner round. Some of his friends are a bit dodgy. They like a drink; well so does he of course, but he'd probably be all right. Will he do?'

'Sorry love. Doesn't sound like my sort of tenant. Thanks for letting me know.'

It was Christmas Eve and Aunt Doris was off to her friend's for a few days. She kissed her good-bye and went on the internet to search for jobs. There were no jobs in the public sector; in fact very few jobs at all. She was beginning to feel a little down, when she went to make a cup of tea and opened the fridge. Aunt Doris had stocked it up with all sorts of treats and had cooked her a Christmas dinner that she would eat tomorrow. She was not on her own. She had some good friends and her Aunt had come up trumps. She'd never be able to tell her Aunt what it had been like trying to stretch out her little bit of money for three months and how hungry she'd been some days; somehow though she'd find a way to pay her back for her kindness.

The next day Jodie decided to have a relaxing day, reading and watching TV. She'd get on with the decorating tomorrow. She planned to tackle the hall. The high ceiling would be a challenge, but she'd find a way. She went to pull the curtains in the lounge and behind them Jodie found a very odd shaped present with her name on. 'I'll go and make some tea and toast and then I'll open my present,' she thought. 'What could it be? How lovely to have a surprise on Christmas day.'

The spidery handwriting told her it was from her Aunt. The red and green paper had some old sticky tape on. Jodie smiled. She tore off the paper and found a small box of chocolates, a paint brush and a list. Unrolling the list her Aunt had written:

You're welcome to live with me as long as you like. I love the company. I know you are desperately trying to find a job but why don't you think of becoming a painter and decorator. You are very good at it and a lot of my friends have jobs wanting to be done. Starting your own business would be fun and I'm sure we could share my car until you get on your feet. I've written down what jobs they want done and what they would be willing to pay. Give it some thought and have a lovely day. Aunt Doris xx

Jodie laughed out loud. 'What a ridiculous idea!' But as the day went on, the more she thought about it and the more she liked it.

So if you see a pink van with this message on the side, be sure to give her a wave.

Jodie's Make Over – *No room too small to be made beautiful.*
> **Tel: 01 666 5454**
> www.jodiesmakeover.co.uk

It was the best Christmas present ever.

The Original Species

Elinor balanced the book on her head until she was far enough down the stepladder to land the book on the desk. A small cloud of dust immediately went up in the air and was visible in the light streaming in from the window. Taking a seat at the large oak desk, she opened the book carefully and began hunting for a zebrule. Images of sepia coloured animals and carefully drawn black and white ones, swept before her eyes.

'There it is,' she thought, 'the hybrid of a zebra and a mule, half covered with stripes. It was just like the picture her colleague Mike had sent her. These accidents of nature happened now and again, in the wild, but it meant the creature was quite rare.

Having identified the animal wouldn't help Mike a lot. A local tribe, in Africa where he was working, wanted to kill the animal for its coat, but Mike with his passion for animals would find a way to protect it. She had no doubt about that.

Elinor continued to browse through the old book. She loved it. Being a zodiographer herself, she enjoyed seeing how her grandfather and his generation had meticulously recorded every new species they could find and many had made names for themselves in the process. If the photographs were unclear or nobody had been able to take one they'd drawn the animals seen on their research trips with amazingly accurate detail. There was little chance of finding new species these days, but as she loved the study of animals and nature for its own sake, she was not bothered about becoming famous.

She flicked her blonde hair out of her eyes and decided that she'd wash and clean up the specimen that Mike had sent her, currently residing in the spare freezer in the cellar. Knowing him he'd have bagged and crated it up as soon as it had been killed by the locals, probably having to give them a bribe so that he could keep it. If she cleaned it up now, she could photograph it and check her books tonight to see if she could identify it. Tomorrow she'd go into the University's lab. The creature would have sufficiently defrosted to be put through the scanner machine. Then she'd be able to see its insides without cutting it up and it could be preserved for future study.

Donning some clean green scrubs, which she'd inherited from her days working as a vet, she secured a mask over her mouth and set up her mobile phone as a Dictaphone. She slipped on latex gloves and went to lift the crated package from the chest freezer. It was cold in the cellar where she worked. Not quite so cold that you could see your breath, but uncomfortable nevertheless. Prizing off the outer wooden casing, Elinor unwrapped the creature. She poured a bowl of cold water and using a sterile sponge, cleaned the small rodent like body. It was the size of a squirrel and its eyes were unnervingly wide open. She felt almost as if she was being watched. She examined the creature carefully but there was no sign of a wound. Perhaps it had died of natural causes.

The room was uncannily quiet as she photographed the creature with the beautiful gem like eyes. Her new digital camera, although small, was of an excellent quality. The camera reflected in the creature's eyes making them appear like emeralds.

Having photographed every angle, she was quite sure that she'd not seen this animal before. She went to leave the cellar, but on glancing back saw its forlorn little body lying starkly on the bench, so she wrapped it in a wodge of cotton wool and placed it carefully in half of the wooden crate. In her usual untidy manner she left the bowl of water on the bench and the gloves discarded by its side.

From the starkness of the cellar room she was pleased to return to her large comfortable, warm study. Three walls were lined with bookshelves, floor to ceiling. The fourth wall contained the fire, which was lit in the grate and was the focal point of the room. Nearby was a dark green leather sofa. Elinor ignored that. She heaved the antique book from her desk so that it was by the fire. Then she picked up a crimson embroidered cushion, and stuffed it between her back and the sofa and started to hunt for the creature through the yellowed pages. The book provided no answers, which meant that Elinor had to hit the internet to continue her search. She worked late into the night, but with no luck.

Living alone in her small house had never bothered Elinor. She was quite happy with her own company and a good book, but as she went upstairs to bed she suddenly felt for the first time that she was not entirely alone.

In the morning she cradled her coffee cup in her hands to warm them as she went downstairs to the cellar. She picked up the other half of the crate and placed it carefully over the creature. Then she went to throw away the water in the bowl but there was none. Elinor shrugged and picked up the gloves to bin them but they fell apart in her hand. 'Mice,' she thought and left the room with the little box.

The lab was bright and white and immaculate. It was a privilege to have access to such facilities. She'd booked an hour in the scanner suite, to examine her specimen and as it remained unidentified she hoped the inner image would provide some sort of clue as to what it was.

'Well that's odd,' she thought as she opened the box. 'It's lying on its front but I placed it on its back. Oh I'm completely mad; I must've opened the box upside down.'

She took out the little body and placed it on the scanner. Then she went into the next room to watch the images come through. It was nothing like the insides of anything she'd seen before. The images started at the feet but when they reached what should have been the digestive area there were two heart like organs. These images were not clear.

'Oh are you scanning a live animal?' Nadine, the laboratory assistant, asked her.

Elinor was about to say no, when she realized that maybe she was. As soon as the machine switched off she went in and picked up the inert body to feel if it was warm, but it was cold. She looked again into the reflective eyes.

'You're going to kill me, aren't you?' a voice said inside her head. It was a shock to realize the creature was communicating with her. She found her hands were sweating and wiped them down her jeans.

'No, but where are you from?' she asked.

'I live a far distance from your Earth. I come from one of the moons of the planet you call Jupiter. You will want to cut me up to see how I work. I have seen it in your science books.'

'Jupiter? I didn't think life was possible there. Oh my goodness I have so many questions. I can't

146

believe you're alive. Oh this is so exciting. I do want to know how you survive and oh I have loads to ask. Listen I'm going to put you back in the crate and take you back to my home. There are some here who might want to have a good look at you, so it'll be safer there. Once we get home we'll decide how to help you.'

Quickly Elinor downloaded the scanned images onto a pen drive and deleted them from the university's computer. She carried the crate under one arm and passed Nadine on the way out.

'Did you find out what it was?' Nadine asked.

'Yes, it was a common African rodent. I'm just going to take it home and write it up for Mike as part of his visit. See you next week.'

On arriving home, Elinor went into her library and undid the crate. She lifted out the creature.

'What can I do to make you comfortable and well?' she asked.

'I will recover slowly as I wake up properly. We sleep for many of your years at a time and as we sleep our body temperature falls below zero,' she heard. 'I have had so little sleep.'

'Would you like some water?'

'Yes and thank you. And I want to know why you're not going to kill me and become famous, like your grandfather for discovering new species?'

'You're a living creature, just like me and I write about animals because they fascinate me. You could tell me all about yourself and where you live and I promise I'll never publish the information until we've got you safely home.'

'If you publish then my home won't be safe.'

'What if you tell me about your life and I write it as a story, not as a fact? Nobody will ever guess that

147

I've really met an alien and I can always change the planet you really come from.'

And the little creature, with deep soulful eyes, looked into Elinor's crystal blue ones and saw the same love of life that he had. Both scientists in their different ways, they told their stories to worlds that listened fascinated, but never for one moment suspected the truth.

If you've enjoyed this book you might enjoy other books by Penny Luker.

Missing – *Short stories for adults*
The Mermaid - *Short stories for adults*

The Truth Finder - *Fantasy novels*
The Visualizer
The Healer

Nature's Gold - *Poetry*
Autumn Gold - *Poetry*
Shadows of Love - *Poetry*

Children's Books

The Green Book *a gentle, magical story*
Chapter book

Tiny Tyrannosaurus *a gentle, magical story*
Chapter book

Pablo the storytelling bear, a magical Chapter book

Desdemona. The dragon without any friends.
Picture book

Read more of Penny Luker's writing at:

www.pennyluker.wordpress.com

Printed in Great Britain
by Amazon